Spirits of Place

Bentley Le Baron

Denman Island, BC, V0R 1T0, 1999

CONTENTS

ACKNOWLEDGEMENTS

Thanks for inspiration, ideas, and some lovely lines. I am sure there are others whom, at this moment, I am not remembering by name, but to whom I am none the less grateful.

Armond, Dale de

The Holy Bible, King James Version

Bly, Robert

Burnett, Frances H.

Cummings, E. E.

Dickinson, Emily

Frost, Robert

Gimbutas, Marija

Graves, Robert

Inanna

Kabir

Kane, Sean

Lao-Tzu

Lawrence, D. H.

Lopez, Barry

Oliver, Mary

Ovid

Rilke, R. M.

Shelley, P. B.

Snyder, Gary

Thoreau, H. D.

INTRODUCTION: SPIRITS OF PLACE

Look, there in the spot of sun on the rock wall, next to the violets. First snake of the season. The immortal coil.

Do you ever think about what Yahweh says to the serpent in the garden?

"Because thou hast done this,
thou art cursed...." etc.

The curse is a heavy one, and most people remember it: "upon thy belly shalt thou go..." and "...it shall bruise thy head...etc." But no record, not in my Bible at any rate, of what the serpent says back to Yahweh. Quite curious!

Is it a one-way conversation? Is the serpent speechless? I don't think so. We know the serpent has a voice because he has just had an intimate and persuasive conversation with Eve, and given the difference of opinion between him and Yahweh, you would hardly expect him to let the matter drop. He too is a god, after all, and he has had an established reputation from long before young Yahweh comes on the scene. So the question is what does the serpent reply to Yahweh's curse. I imagine something like this: "Hey laddie, I've just done nine turns around the cosmic egg and I can use a rest. So if you want to play Lord for a while please be my guest. I'll take a nap here in the sunshine.

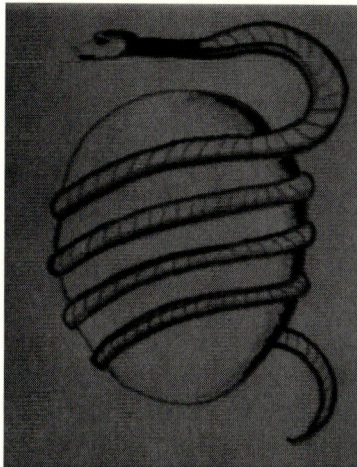

Much later there is the story of the disciples waking Jesus when they are afraid of being swamped by the raging storm. Jesus talks to the wind and the waves:

"Peace," he says. "Be still."

And they comply; they calm right down. Again, there is no record of what the wind and water may have said to Jesus, on this or some other occasion, but I find myself imagining a conversation, perhaps when they are alone with him. "Come out into the desert for a few days," wind will be saying. "I have a few things to show you."

Of course all this was a long time ago. For some centuries now, it has not been in the mainstream of fashion to converse with creatures, still less with such inarticulate beings as wind or waves. You might not want to let people overhear such a conversation, lest they think you balmy. But of late it seems as if it has become socially acceptable again to honor the gods and goddesses, even to talk to them. Especially if you call it prayer.

There is, you cannot help but notice, a burgeoning literature and art reviving the very ancient deities--especially the goddesses--and I find it fascinating. Who would not be horribly repulsed by old Kali-Ma, of the monster teeth and the apron of skulls? Who would not be in thrall to great Tiamat, the one who births dragons? I suppose I have always hoped to lie next to sea-foam Aphrodite, voluptuous incarnation of all loves and lusts, not to mention eternal springtime. And, with my fellow potters (east and west) I have come to honor Nammu and Nu Wa, the original sculptresses, of us, from clay.

So, too, the old stories are full of the creator gods, leaning out over the earth from their celestial chariots, pushing us into our appointed places, with thunderbolt or Holy Word which no one can withstand. There is mighty Ophion, the cosmic serpent, coiling around the world egg. Who could ignore Shiva, of the monumental phallus, or black Tezcatlipoca, reflecting in his smoking mirror the universal catalogue of tricks, travesties, and savage rites. And there are Marduk and Yahweh, the jealous gods, who insist on "Only Me!"

But if Kali is the Maha Devi--which is to say, the Great Goddess--who masticates entire armies (chariots, horses, elephants, all) in a casual, carnal mouthful, perhaps by now, thousands of mortal and immortal armies later, she is a bit puffed up. Meanwhile, down close to earth, there is also the Grami Devi--that is, the local goddess--the one who lives in the village with the people, the one who is known by vulgar and tender names: Old Fishy Smell; She of the Amorous Backside. She is the one who receives the everyday affections of ordinary folk and, I suppose, returns their affections.

West Africans have a charming name for the little household deity who helps with domestic things. They call him "The One You Meet Everywhere." He is a brother of the Neolithic "little gods," small enough to fit in the hand, domestic deities of hearths and fields.

Mostly I know them from books of art and archeology, but one I know face to face, the one who lives on the bookshelf under my window. A friend brought him to me from Mexico decades ago. He is a dignified, chipped and faded little fellow--once, long ago, brick red, now gray--and he looks at me with his unblinking owly eyes, from a flattened tortilla face, each time I sit down at my desk. Did I tell you he sometimes talks? We say a few simple things to each other. "How old are you, little man?" I ask him.

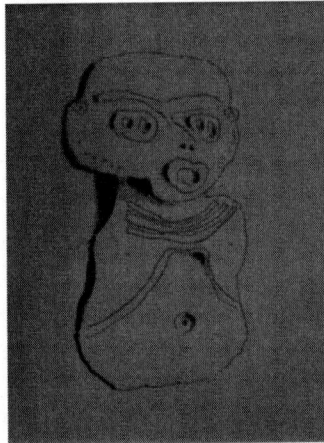

-- *No importa. Bastante.*
"What have you seen, Abuelito?"
-- *Mais, frijoles,...trabajo....*
"Where did you live?"
-- *Con una familia.*
"What did you do?"
-- *Les dí consuelo, en los tiempos difíciles.*

"I comforted them," he says, "in their hard times."
It is enough.

In so few words I am there; a village life enfolds me, planting, hoeing, harvesting.

I am taken further back, many millennia, by the astonishing "little goddesses" of the Paleolithic: lovely, lovingly fashioned beings in bone,

6

stone, ivory and clay. Nowadays, it seems fashionable to represent them as the earliest images of the continent bestriding Great Goddess, and I suppose in a sense they are that, but is it possible that in this mirror we glimpse our own propensity for inflation? Why not imagine that these tiny artifacts are images of concrete female experiences: at *this* shelter-cave, in *this* stream for gathering and washing, through *this* birthing trauma and ecstasy?

However that may be, I begin to notice a certain weariness in myself, as if in conjuring up the great deities I may be taking myself a bit grandly. I would rather make a place for the down-home antics of coyote and raven, those nutcase transformers--it would be grandiose to imagine them gods--whose efforts at creation, of worlds and people and all the other stuff, are more likely to bring down mischief than majesty, and who are perpetually in jams of their own flavor. We do not so much honor these two, as laugh with them. Like pre-adolescents, some of their favorite jokes are about bodily functions. And, like us adults, they are forever pretentious, repeatedly slapped down, and apparently unable to learn much.

Yes, it is raven I would like to talk to. Or to serpent, or wind.

It is this bruising of their head by our heel that wearies me. This, I take it, is how the curse has come down to us. The despoiling of brother and sister species. The despoiling of waters and winds. Yes, even the air, that taken-for-granted soul-stuff we pull into our bodies, breath by breath.

I notice myself wanting to cultivate reverence, as if that might help me get things right. But, perhaps a bit like Kali, I am trying for too big a bite. Perhaps what is needed (by me, at any rate) is more like courtesy and conversation. For today, I will try for these. And, if Raven has his way with me, I may get a little irreverence.

So I bring my attention down from cosmic realms to the neighbors I live with. From the whole earth to the dirt-under-my-feet. I honestly do not know what there is for you, or me--any of us--to do about the big machine which is running so magnificently amok, except to stand back, and marvel.

What I have at my doorstep, this morning, is an almost irrelevant scrap of remnant forest. A stream, the rowdy, randy bark of sea lion bulls, and the smell of rain. For long I have loved them, but perhaps I have not taken time enough, lately, to talk with them. Today I will listen, and pick up some conversations I have been neglecting, with the spirits of this place.

Come with me, friend. Get your hat and boots and we'll go out.

1. ENTRANCES

This is my first awareness of a possible place.

Through a green screen, from a narrow road, a glimpsed opening, beckoning with light. Too small to be called a meadow, not significant really. But wide as a sliver of dream-stuff; big enough, I think, to plant a person, and a row of sweet peas. I will push through, and look.

No path.

A scrabble through salmonberry; shadowed movement of water just narrow enough to jump; grandfather firs, sword ferns, then late-summer bracken, and tangled grasses. A slender, slanted, tower of sun.

Listen. At earth level, listen. "Ears of my ears, awake."

Capillary sounds. Carapace scrape and rustle. Humus humming. A membrane stretches, becomes transparent. Pass through it. Yes . . . here.

First task, a foot bridge.

Clear a pull-off for a car, at roadside. Open a miniature switch-back path to the creek; line it with oyster shells for night-walking. Cut slender poles (astonishing filaments of flexed fixed energy); place them horizontal, with cedar crosspieces, and rough arch-over, faintly Japanese, without formality.

Evening and morning. They take pleasure, and call it good.

Call this the first, and still favorite, entrance.

Today, another season, a dozen years later, I am here at water-side just to say good morning. Stream at ease, as usual, no hurry. She knows the end of her journey is only minutes away.

Bridge, like me, shows scrapes, sags, makes creaking noises. We both acknowledge punky spots. But he jokes that in these days of redundancy and early retirement he sure is glad to still have his job. One day at a time, and all that.

Spirits of walking, spirits of feet. Pause here. Low speech, barely audible. I lay myself down, with an ear to the path. Something about bliss, and timelessness . . . ? No, wait! Make that blisters, and untidiness . . . .

I can sink lower. I will say something to the hidden-under things, those always present beings, the invisible single and several cells. But what? Suddenly I feel stupid, tongue-tied. What *does* one say to one's original ancestor (to the one who's been everywhere, done everything, to the one who has made the long voyage, sailed every sea) that isn't parochial and callow?

Then I do think of something. I want to ask what it feels like to divide into two. Mitosis--tell me about it! Is it fun? Is it sexy? Strenuous? Or quite ho-hum after all those billions of times?

A possible answer, from some dimly remembered place in the mud:

> . . . when it blows, there is only wind;
> when it rains, there is only wet;
> when the clouds pass, sun shines through. . . .

I think I have to go now. Tomorrow I may come back, looking for an easier conversation. With the ones who don't usually mock me: maybe the gloriously golden-gowned skunk cabbage, or the newt with startling orange underbelly . . . .

* * *

There is a second entrance.

Begin at the smell of salt, and the sinuous line of tangled treasure-wood. Turn your back to a sister island; turn from sensuous fingers of wind, and the wide shout of gulls; come up, away, from the female curve of the bay.

Turn right, pass the gate and garden of the good neighbors, turn left at the tall hemlocks, then again right (after the glacial boulder) into what was once a lane, before these rambunctious, swift-springing, adolescent firs declared it theirs. . . and then we took issue with them and made it again a lane.

May we come in by this way?

This way . . . in through the folk tale. Enter the faery wood, into the always, the archetypal "clearing in the forest"--where the old hag lives. And here we are, time-warped, vortexed, contracted: in from her expanse, into her enclosure, suddenly wombed.

Interior fastness.

Microcosmic *vestigium* of ancient Arkadia. "Taken as the ideal region of rural contentment."

Modest modern refuge for the memory of the disreputable, the smelly goat-god. Honeysuckle and blueberries luxuriate where he danced. Is that a faintly lingering vibration of the archaic shepherd's pipe? Of course not. Lingering echo, perhaps, of dream music? Of rippling through the rushes; of sweet Syrinx' cries, panic, and ecstasy? Such romantic imaginings! A modern sensibility must not credit nymph-glimpses, still less make votive offering to the Lady of the Wild Things. Smile--but never really mind the flickering fancies of a vanished, banished childhood.

In the beginning, I simply sat, with bee-loud silence in my ears.

Eventually, I roused myself, burned a great tangle of brush and bramble at the edge of the glade, then built a small house where the ashes lay.

Like the Vedics of another continent, I asked for a blessing--or at least the acquiescence--of Vritra, deep coiling one, as I pinned the earth for a foundation corner. A small brown snake flickered into the light, looked over the ashes, and was gone.

In five cut lengths, like small whales, we moved a massive cedar nurse log, and built a kiln-shed where her dreaming had lain, where it still lies, and will, I suppose, unmoved, for another 350 years. A blown down maple stood smartly up again, grasped the end of a roof beam and supported it skyward.

So, today, in a clearing within the hag's forest is a house, a workshop, a garden. So far, she has permitted it. She is, it seems, as generous as she is implacable.

It has been observed that all forests are one. Every forest, even a remnant such as this, echoes the first forest. You know, the wide-spreading forest, the one that received the first mystery from rock and water, robed it in primal green, and placed it deep in cell memory, when the story was young. I guess this is why every forest is the hag's forest. Why we enter any forest at her pleasure, and our peril.

Our bounded, tamed, domesticated woodlots seem to us innocuous, and transparent. Look again. Listen again. Sit very still . . . lie . . . sink, as the fawn does, into shadow. Slowly, slowly, raise the head. Turn it, imperceptibly; and look over the left shoulder.

Every forest is a forest of eyes.

The ancient forest, the one which is always dangerous, cannot be cut down.

The old self, the one suckled by wolf or bear, cannot be lost. In darkness, without compass or star, a traveler knows the north side of a tree, by its touch, or by its smell.

Enter a forest. Watch for her brambled hidden hut, at the edge.

Enter a relationship, or a life's work. The hag is there. Listen for her footstep.

* * *

Come now, I have one more way-in to show you. Here, on the far side of the clearing, is the third, the ordinary, and now the well-worn, entrance.

This area had been newly logged. Look . . . massive stumps, lurking under this lush of twining green. For several seasons we gathered slash here, for firewood

I remember how we led this driveway in, a meandering way, on a tether string of October mornings. Planted these little redemptions: lilacs, walnuts, hazelnuts, to make a welcome. Planted flowering plums, and cherries, to greet The Guest.

So now, when humans come, they mostly come in by car, down this drive.

What do they see?

Trees, then a clearing, a cluster of buildings, daffodils (if it is March, or April), a courtyard with sculpted figures.

Perhaps, on occasion, visitors may think they've glimpsed the horned one. I have seen them rub their eyes, or look quickly away. If they imagine that they hear conversations--the whispers, the muffled laughter-- they mostly do not mention it.

Some do.

When I go by car--out into the community, or for a town trip--I come back in by this entrance. What do I see? My eyes see what they see, the welcome sights of home.

And there is another eye.

There is another I.

There is the quick one, not bounded by this body;

the one who moves inside the song, an impulsive cantata; the one
who dissolves outward like smoke, ahead of me,
meets the rooted,
fierce, exuberant beings who live here. . . tree frogs, mahonia,
wood bugs. . .
flows into the interstices of their bark and sap;
the one who greets, gestures, capers in motley,
hoots, whispers . . . a stillness. . . thanks.

There is another eye. . . .

the one who watches

from the shadow.

2. HERON

Is it true, old soul, that you have given birth to rivers, and to silence? Is it true that, if you choose, you can enter liquid autumn and leave no ripple? That you can stand and cast no shadow?

How fragile, the artifact of time. So laps my thought against a quiet strand, each time I watch you, dusk-draped uncle, balanced there, timeless--out of time--at tide's edge. Where you have stood, Zen poised, as ever you have stood--

precise

patient

pitiless

--while we, with industrious appetite, ate millennia, invented ourselves, excavated ourselves (layer by layer), broke through tough temporal crusts, to shape our conscious crystal now.

How fallible, how deceptive an artifact, our human attribution.

I notice the shades through which I imagine I glimpse you, the permeable metaphors in which I think to net you. You are ancestral, archaic, prehistoric, so I want to say. But you stand aside. I see that you bear no relation at all to time, early, or late.

You are inscrutable, self-possessed, opaque. So I imagine. Can I slow and pace this mind-rhythm to your point of rapier stillness, can I for a moment pause? Then perhaps you will turn and explain yourself, tell me how these musings miss the mark. But I expect you will minutely shift your shade-sharp feather-weight, lift, and away.

Even in my forest clearing I am gifted once, several times in a season, gifted out of time, by the shudder of your sea-born presence moving over me. I feel, before I hear, the Serengeti drum under each crested arm. And then the edge of voice that could be the echo of torrents, could be the clash and grind of great machinery, from coal pits, or threshing fields, except that it is earlier and chthonic, perhaps a species of tectonic groan, signaling eruption or quake.

Looking up. A familiar shiver merging dread with joy and excitation, eternity with a moment of glass. The pterodactyl silhouette of you against sky. Heavy, low, deliberate. Two thrusts, three, a soaring turn at the edge of trees, and gone. Breathe, breathe mortal breath. Slide back into body. Touch grass.

* * *

When I came to this place, they told me there had been a heron rookery in that stand of second growth fir. There, across the creek, past the cedar snag and the old maples. I went over to have a look. I saw the remnants of nests, tattered bundles of sticks, a hundred feet up, more, over my head. You have moved, you and your mates, from this nest place, probably several years ago. You found a spot inland, I guess. I think there are still places where you can roost, for a while yet, behind a green veil.

They said that your young, unfeathered, sometimes fell from the nest, might be encountered just here where we stand, at the bottom of this cool forest well: might be upright, on spindle-sticks, pale, ghostly, fragile as fungi. Helpless. Hopeless. Waiting.

I glance around. The filtered light thickens, turns cold. As I move away, seeking sun, I watch where I place my feet.

* * *

2

Against rock, and drift, and tide, where you are familiar as a fixture, I take you almost for granted. But one day I glance out of my window and there you come, strolling down the hot summer driveway-- owning it--toward me.

I am startled, as by an apparition. Up close, you are twice as tall, and (at ease on those impossible pipes) twice as strange.

In my left eye I see you as a contemplative, walking for health and meditation. A Hegelian perhaps, or a rabbi. Will you stop in for a cool drink? Do you have any priestly jokes?

In my right eye you are no uncle at all. Not cousin, not ancestor, not school-master, but thoroughly alien: an improbable invader--though no doubt you were here first--from a deeply foreign star.

I want to laugh with delight, to welcome you, to say how I am honored that you walk the path to my door. And a shadow passes over, a premonition. I do not think you intend to speak but, in any case, I think I would dread to hear the words you would utter.

Suddenly, in a prodigal froth of passion, I am angry with you. I will spring upon you, grapple you down, force you to say what you want of me, wrestle with you as Jacob with the angel, until you bless me. I grasp you by that scaly up-raised claw, seize that predatory coil of neck. I shall not let you go until you speak to me--of far off, fearful cataclysms, of fishy gods, of hates and fates and a case of indigestion, of what you will-- but speak!

Now I am closing my hands on un-roughed air; my ears are ringing with emptiness. And you!--you are untouched, you notice me not, not even the modest acknowledgment of disdain! Oh you, Great Prophet, Great Pretender: aloof, serene, intent on your intent, whatever it may be.

Now you are walking here, and I am gone. Studio gone. Garden gate gone. House dissolved into memory. Gone.

Alders, where once was road. Only a trail remains, the bended kind made by beasts, not men.

Deliberately...foot lifted, paused, placed ... the other lifted, held... you walk here.

3. FROG

Even here, on the rocky rim of a continent, washed by rough Pacific hands, we watch and listen for spring.

Winter is not, for us, a crystal palace, but this verdant house of scrubbed boughs, under a chiaroscuro wind. We mark the Solstice night with a walk through a black swash of rain, and remember to remember sun.

There will be false promises. Plum blossoms in December, or primulas in January. We are not fooled. There are inundations yet to come.

Someone looks for robins. Yesterday she saw one; today her garden is awash with them.

Another waits for geese, for the moment when that implacable banner of sound streams over us like a voice of destiny, fast and low.

Someone says: it is the red glow of the rose bramble and Osier Dogwood twigs along the road side. Another says: I watch for those outrageous sunbursts of forsythia. And someone else: Oh! I know it when I smell the herring.

All of these are the stage sets. The props and prompts. The cues.

The small perfect one who announces spring has been tuning up just off stage, there, at the curtain of reeds. There have been preliminary chirps and trills, to find the pitch. There have been single, hesitant, practice notes; then, again, silence. There have even been short warm-up solos, quartets, brief fragments of ensemble pieces. The house stills, hears its breathing, attuned.

Hush.

It is evening, pungent as wet musk, the warmest we have had. A singer opens his throat and finally here it is, a full, confident note. Upstream, a reply, equally confident now, pouring it out, a lusty duet. Another joins in; another, another, until every leaf and blade is singing. Full volume, an answering chorus across the marsh, a third further away; song outspilling, like ornament or ardor, a vibrant astonishing celebration of sound. We are surrounded, immersed, a stunning cascade of jewels, a rapture. The night is bathed in beauty.

Hyla regilla, Pacific tree frog. Mating season. Resonating. With your vocal sac so passionately extended, I think you could jump into your own throat. It is said that you sing so hard in one night that you have to rest for a week before you can sing again.

The book says it is the guys singing to the girls. I think you are singing to the universe. More precisely, the universe, the whole flung spangle of stars, is pouring itself--a profligate exuberance--through you.

Not every listener hears with the ears of millennia. Some speak of cheeps, peeps, whistles, clicks, and croaks. I hear the oldest music. Probably about 400 million years old, as these things are counted. I imagine the original song in the world sung by a frog, by that early bold adventurer who first pulled himself up out of water onto earth, who eyed the first leaf, climbed the first stem, and--who knows?-- trembled with the first ecstasy. In such heroic tiny ones as these was music born, and the gift offered, outward, onward, a shower of light, until it came to us.

Thanks, little eloquent elf, pulsing emerald, big as a blossom, with your reckless wardrobe, with your impy grin. Praise, for your Ode to Joy.

* * *

And thanks for the dazzlement to the eye, quick-change adept. Camouflage artist. Now you see me, now you don't. Temperature, light, moisture, texture. Is it also desire? Or fear? I'd blend too, if I knew how.

"Jumping one," the Romans called you.

Climbing one, I call you. Cling to anything, with your fat round sticky padded toes: cling to branches and stalks, to leaves, to life. Climb the post, climb the wall. Press the sculpture in my garden with the carved precision of your soft beast body. Decorate the *tokonoma* of my imagination. Be welcome. Be as beautiful as you are.

You jaunty tree frogs and your 4000 species of froggish cousins (minute as a housefly, plump as a platter) where under heaven did you buy your tropical paintbox, and those scandalous brushes? Do you sit, day by day, in your leafy boudoirs, in your high-fashion stream-side salons, just decorating each other, devising ever more shocking juxtapositions of campy color, out-punking the gaudy punks?

I guess you begin modestly enough with your palette of greens-- deep forest green, pale pea green, jade, olive, moss--then on to green with brown spots and borders, green with buff belly, green with white T-shirt, green with black eye patch, or, why not all together? And that is just warming up.

Now throw away all precedent, all restraint. Go for the brilliant orange toes, the ruby eyeballs. Crimson butt, pink panties, lavender lace: if I can imagine it, a frog, somewhere, is wearing it. Let's do tawny tiger stripes, golden spice sprinkles, purple trousers, and maroon chin blush.

Now shake the kaleidoscope for the colors of peril. Let's do death-dart yellow, and blast-furnace red. Do them with ominous blues: steel-electric-midnight-murder blues. Not to mention poison plum.

My hands are pruning a dwarf apple tree, and my head is skipping about the planet: Costa Rica, Surinam, all those exotic hot-houses where the swipe of an arrow-point across a frog's flaunting flank is enough to paralyze the monkey who will presently be a hunter's dinner. But just now, at this apple branch, I am eye to eye with you, and your colors are neither poisonous nor outrageous. Color you elegant rain. Color you streambank, or river. Colors of gardens, rice fields, cool sleep.

* * *

I bring my monstrous face close to your miniature one. You do not move, do not seem to mind. The glow on your face is beatific, bordering on smug. Submerged in your passions, I presume. Passion memories, or dreams.

I feel myself pulled closer, until the ball of your eye is huge, until your eye fills mine completely. And your eye is your whole self; your great round eye is your universe, invading mine. I look into the liquid globe of you. I liquefy myself. I slide into your pool.

In a fluid world, I float... drift... kick... luxuriate. Weightless, silken, sensuality.

My own froggy female shimmers into view, looming large, lusty, webbed, utterly amphibian, utterly compelling. We drift together, embrace, entwine, consummate, kick... languid kicks, of contentment.

I am swimming in nectar and ambrosia. I am immersed in pleasure.

I merge with the ancient sea.

I become the ancient song.

The world dissolves itself into song, singing about singing. All is song-stuff. The gods melt back into music, from whence they were born.

I am the frog as large as the galaxy--I swallow nebulae like flies.

I am a green note in your hand—do I content you?

4. WORMS

Worm.

(Old English. Variations: wyrm, wirm, werm, wurm, virme, vurm.)

A serpent, snake, or dragon. Any animal that creeps, or crawls.

There is a garden, an enclosed, an enchanted place. Each day I inhabit this garden made by our own hands.

To come in to our little garden by the east gate, you must pass under the guard dragon. Coming through the west gate you must stare down a tiger.

* * *

It is said that the entrances to temples are flanked by guardians. Hideous sword-swinging dwarves and demons whose task is the slaying-- no hesitation!--of unworthy seekers. Of course, the pure in heart will walk serenely by these ruffians into the cool, the blessed sanctum of tranquillity.

Perhaps it is as well that I did not go to the temple. I see myself prostrate, scrabbling and clutching at those dread feet like claws. I hear myself piteously wailing.

But there are no such extravagances here. The cherubim who pretend to guard this modest garden appear to be less than efficacious. Birds, branches, spiders, snow--they all take liberties upon the gate dragon. The demon in his snarl is gently mocked by dawn-drenched threads of crystal light, danced from wing-tip to wing-tip. And Tiger! With her butt in the air, she looks more pussycat than savage. So far as anyone can tell, neither one guardian nor the other has yet made any impression on the ghost-footed forest dwellers who, on occasion, slip in and out through gossamer openings only they know, leaving raw stems where beans and broccoli were, and pointy toe-tracks in tell-tale dirt.

How many gardens?

Like the shut-up secret garden on the moor, ours needs no mortal help to come alive each new spring, with pale emerald pins pushing through delicately decayed traceries of yester-leaves.

Like the ever-shimmering mythical garden, eastward—the "first" garden--ours has a tree with fruit "in the midst thereof", and a serpent. Several serpents, I should say. Sometimes a small congress of sun-seeking snakes, sudden un-braiding, sliding shiverly side-wise. Each time, again and again, I nod to the poet who could put this shiver into words:

> But never met this fellow,
> Attended or alone,
> Without a tighter breathing,
> And zero at the bone.

Out of the zero, recovering courtesy, I gather a thank-thought: narrow cousin, I am honored by your persistent presence in our garden, delighted to share with you this short bake of August, and I appreciate your diet of slugs.

It is marvelously, mercifully true: our garden is mostly un-munched by the slimy sisters. Many gardeners on this island wage monster battles with slugs but we do not. Oh yes, we uncover a few tiny glue-globs between lettuce leaves and the occasional mucilaginous grandfather murdering a marigold. But mostly we are un-slugged and I think we have you narrow fellows to thank.

* * *

How many gardens?

Sing with the poet of the garden--and the orchard--of the gods.

2

And out of the ground
made the Lord God to grow
every tree that is pleasant to the sight,
and good for food.

In an ancient language, the garden is *pardes,* the same root for
paradise. Persian *pairidaeza,* an enclosed garden of delights. Enclosed.
Contained. Cultivated. A garden is no longer wild: not the wide raucous
sunrise of awesome surprises, but already the deepening afternoon of
ordered anticipations. And guards, always guards, at the entrances.

This newly established trio of order--Gods, and Guarding, and
Gardens--wanders in to the oasis like tribesmen out of the desert,
mingling blood and settling down. Order comes in from that other, that
primordial garden, the one that needed no gates or walls, the one that
asked for no cultivation. Creates this new garden, this deliberate garden,
the one made with cunning intentions. Plants the corn and the new social
establishment in the same kernel. Plants the village. Plants the town, and
the city.

Who sings in such an early garden? Inanna sings her praise song
to her other, to Dumuzi, the gardener, to Dumuzi, the green man, the
honey man, the beloved:

He has sprouted; he has burgeoned;
He is lettuce planted by the water.
He is the one my womb loves best.

My well-stocked garden of the plain,
My barley growing high in its furrow,
My apple tree which bears fruit up to its crown,
He is lettuce planted by the water.

How many gardens? Sing the Song of Songs. How many lovers
look into the mirror of gardened earth, to find the *pairidaeza* of the body?

He sings: A garden enclosed is my sister, my
spouse;
a spring shut up, a fountain sealed.

Thy plants are an orchard of
pomegranates,
with pleasant fruits...
with all the chief spices....

She sings: Awake, O north wind;
and come, thou south;
blow upon my garden, that the spices thereof may flow
out.
Let my beloved come into his garden,
and eat his pleasant fruits.

* * *

Here at home in the haiku garden made by our hands I am on my
knees between asparagus and rhubarb, pulling pertinacious sorrel,
chucking chick-weed. My beloved, across from me, squats with
strawberries and garlic. It is noon. For these brief hours, between morning
shade and afternoon shade, the garden is a sunny canyon. Our bodies
absorb the heat and return it, damply glowing.

We note yet again the perennial muddle. In too much shade, the
corn and squashes sulk. Potatoes debauch in the compost box, but simper
where we plant them. And we, foolish peasants, have all but assassinated
these royal peonies with an overdose of herring roe. But the cosmos love
it--they are eight feet tall--and there will be a fine crop of blueberries.

As in other seasons, I am entranced again by you baby firs amongst beets and peas. Instant up-springing exuberant youngsters: a couple of inches, six inches, sky reaching, sturdy, belonging here. Soft-spiky ones, I know this is your space, your place of roots, cambium, and ancestors. An intimate corner of your kitchen, which we presume, for a moment, to cultivate, as if it could be anything but wild. I see how confidently you will reclaim it when we have quit. Soon I will lay my body here and it shall be succulent for you. Meanwhile, forgive us our trespasses.

I pull out the little firs. A few I leave, they are so irresistibly green. (I will pull them out later.)

Seaweed from the beach, by the wheelbarrow. A load or two of composted fish, of horse dung. A pail of wood ash. This opened sandy orifice receives them eagerly, all, as it now receives my fingers. It is warm, loose, pubic: pungent as a casserole. There is eating here, big appetite, below this table.

The soil is a slow, voluptuous mouth, and, by the fingertips, I am sucked into it. Already these greedy fingers are thinning, thrusting, threading, extending, burrowing. I shall let them go, on their worming way, into this opulent musk.

I shall make myself round and slender, and slide in after them.

24

5. EAGLE

The eagles are chittering again this morning, very loud, very animated, not far from my studio.

Have you listened to them when they are intent on something really important? What is it--the whole herring fleet has just sailed off the edge of the world, or a gull has been elected Prime Minister? They natter on rapid-fire and vociferous, a cocktail party at an aeronautical convention. I love hearing it. The sharp-edged clicks like snapping their beaks together, the whistling notes, the shrieks and melodious open-throat tones intermingling. It always gives me that keen-edged wake-up feeling.

Love talk, that's what I'll bet. Thinking about nesting and making babies. Or they know the herring will soon be here, and already they are telling fish stories. Or both.

Yesterday on one of the eagle snags along the channel, on a branch where you usually see one there were two, snuggled up as cozy as you please. A few times I've seen six or seven in that tree but usually spaced out on different branches at different levels. So when I see a couple of them rubbing up against each other I start to think mating season. Before long they will be clasping claws in the air, spiraling together in freefall, breaking apart to wheel up into blue, to do it again... and again. Love dance. Primal energy at play.

* * *

Yes, the spring extravaganza is beginning again, the quickening that will rise to a crescendo.

Herring spawn. Potlatch of the ocean; the great give-away. The gathering of sea lions for the feast. The gathering of eagles.

The only time we may see more eagles together is in the fall when the salmon are gathering to move up the rivers. I've seen them in a huge orgy over at the mouth of the Little Qualicum, maybe a couple of hundred at a time, not to mention the same number of gulls, and an assortment of ravens and other odd bods. The eagles are a sight! Seeing them stand on one leg and use the other to hold up a carcass like an oversize hot dog, while they tear at it with their beaks, is something comical. Before long they get gore all over themselves. Then they get so gorged that they wobble like drunks, and can barely fly. Or maybe they can't. Maybe they just stagger over into the bushes to sleep it off.

One thing I haven't seen is eagles bathing in fresh water, and I'd like to. There is a lake where folks have seen them making a huge splashing, cleaning up. Getting the stickiness off? The rotten smell off? Maybe getting the salt off, after they've been diving for fish out in the chuck.

* * *

I am looking into that other pool to see what it is about eagles that moves so powerfully in our imaginations. Is it too obvious to ask?

The Americans put the eagle on their money and their coat of arms. The Mexicans too. What are they looking for? Before that, the First Nations danced and whistled and drummed the eagle. Before that--all the way back through Rome and Babylon--the head honcho flew the eagle on his standard, presumably to intimidate the other guys.

An eagles is big: that is a start. He spreads his wings more than six feet, wider than most of us can spread our arms.

He sees more than we do. It is said that looking through eagle eyes might be something like looking through twelve power binoculars.

So is it longer sight we are seeking?

An eagle strikes us as powerful, fierce, and intelligent. And--one feels compelled to add--very beautiful. You know how when the light slants just so, in the evening, sometimes against the sky those wings are a black cutout, and that head catches a golden radiance.

We are working in the garden at sundown and one comes in low, skimming over our heads. Who wouldn't feel blessed? Dania says "It is an honor to be in their presence," and I am thinking, yes! people have been having that experience, feeling that, saying that, for hundreds of generations. You can understand how the Sioux, for example, would invoke the eagle and the Great Mystery in a single breath.

I walk out to the south end of the island, to the cliff edge, look over the tops of trees growing half way down the face of it. An eagle sits there, at eye level, so close we can see each other blink, notice each other's thoughts come and go, vibrate with the taut cord that connects us. Oh!— that deliberate regal turn of the head, as he links up with me. There is something intimidating in it, as if he had reached over and struck me an invisible blow in the chest. What is he seeing when he looks over at me? Any power? Any intelligence? Anything resembling blessing, or beauty?

I'm looking for the heart of the matter, and of course I come back to wings. Surely it is the high flying that totally captures us. That a being of our dimension can stride over into that other, can ride that thermal, ride that earth-heat elevator under his pinion, ride until he is an Omega point up there against the blue curtain, a weightless slide of lapping circles in the wind: that's freedom. That is outrageous. Our hearts are plundered by that. Something in us is tugged and pulled to take wing.

Flying fantasies! Is there woman or man, now or ever, who has not dreamed of flying?

I have a vivid dream-image of flying a car. I make it fly. At a whim, fly off the edge of a spectacular coastal road, fly over cliffs, soar out over a miniaturized ocean, with laughable little boy-toy boats, and a tiny toy shoreline, and, when I am ready, I make the car fly down on to the roadway again and drive along as if this were a world of only ordinary wonders. More--even while my impudent car was flying, me in it, I was at the same time way out on a longer string, a transparent Chinese kite, looking down, taking the measure of everything. Of course what stays is the wonder and huge delight of such un-boundedness, that flicking off of weight and sobriety as a single shirt.

Another bright fragment in a book of flying fancies. I am carried frightfully fast and high by the lord of all raptors. He has me in his beak. I cling to his face-feathers, my face up next to his eye, looking in through that round window at a landscape of savage and brilliant joy. My body dangles, pummeled by a jet stream, and I fear I am losing my grip--but I know that with scarcely a ruffle he can dive, faster than I know how to fall, to snatch me up again.

How beloved Ganymede flew! In the claws of eagled Zeus, carried off to bear the nectar cups on Olympus.

How young Icarus flew! Prideful, or rash, he flew too high.

How angels fly! Us, they are, except equipped with pure hearts and luminous wings. Consult any number of frescos by Giotto or Fra Angelico.

So. We mundane things live this urge to be magnificent. To connect with the airy beings. To fly. We search for the words that will lift us and Rilke found them:

> I am circling around God,
> around the ancient tower,
> and I have been circling for a thousand years,
> and I still don't know if I am a falcon, or a storm,
> or a great song.

With such thoughts I was circling when word came that Bill had died, had chosen to wing himself over, and I thought, Ah, yes!--how he was a bit of a high flyer, a self-described *puer*, and now, so abruptly, forcefully, perversely, self-grounded. Wings melted. Too close to the heat.

I thought: "Great exit!" for a devotee of high drama.

I thought: Bill, you rode the big emotions, the stormscapes. Sublime peaks and black holes.

Thoughts cresting thoughts, wind on wave.

How in the last few years Bill's personal quest had transformed: from mind search, to spirit seeking, to soul soaring. How in the last few months he opened his voice to his anima, muse stirred, spoke poetry. Growing new bright wings, I had been thinking: hang gliding, getting the feel of flying with flair. And now--so I pictured him--crashed and burned.

It looked like a kind of courage.

It looked like cop-out, like betrayal.

I had liked the light touch, learning to fly with Bill, and I did not now like being left, a heavy body, contemplating a heavy body.

Last night I sat in his house with his friends, planning a send-off service, a releasing, for Bill and for us, with a scattering of his ashes at the creek he loved. I felt, as we sat there speaking of these things, in that down moment I felt, un-bidden, a yeast rising. Planning a ritual which we imagined Bill would enjoy, and suddenly there he was sitting with us, grinning in his wide hearty way, approving, as audibly as dawn is audible, or evening, or friendship. When I stood, Bill more than stood: he hovered. He floated. In a modest way, you could say he flew. And I saw that he intended to hover around, maybe sit in trees, or on rafters, at least until after we have given ourselves his party. For a flickering minute I had a glimpse of him, mock solemn, helping to sprinkle his own ashes.

So there I was noticing all that, and enjoying all that, getting the joke, and I noticed that I had lightened up, was about an inch off the floor myself.

I asked: who is it, this unbounded one, who enters and lifts us?

Well, I thought, the real flyer isn't Bill, certainly isn't me, may be not even the eagle. There is the one who flies in the meadowlark, the one who flies in the periwinkle, in the tough gray granite, and in me--and who keeps on flying when we sleep. There is the one who all this while has been creeping, and burrowing, and swimming in the sulfurous under-sea, and it is the flying one.

The slug is weightless; the toad hovers like a hummingbird in the pregnant, fragrant afternoon.

The high flyer even now is catacombing the sand under my feet. One by one, we are all sucked in. In a moment we shall be exhaled.

It is said that Eros, the golden-winged, was hatched from a silver egg, laid by black-winged Night, the one before whom even the Olympians stand in awe. Eros created earth, sky, and moon. And the Dark One rules the universe.

6. BEAVER

Of course water would be your *anima*. I see how you are a lover of water, a shaper of water.

In the dry months of summer, before you came, I had been noticing and fretting that my little stream was languishing. She was fading as if thirsting for something. Romance perhaps? Flirtation? Assignations? Anyhow that summer I imagined she might waste quite away. Nested ducks flown. Frogs mute and hidden. Stillness, waiting for the prince who didn't come.

And then you did come. I guess you swam down, some inconspicuous night, from the big swamp. Not such a fabulous journey; no significant mountains to cross, no deserts, as from a distant kingdom. And no one noticed your coming: or, at any rate, I didn't. It must have been in the wet season, when November rains, which you know go on for days and nights, had revived the stream to a kind of ecstasy, fattened her, restored appetite and ardor, transformed her once more--whether she will it or not--into a rollicking Rubenesque, all gurgle and giggle and reaching out with fat wet arms to embrace everyone within reach, cedars, alders, night moons....

She would have loved you right away. I guess she embraced you, gave herself up to you, took you to her bed, invited you to stay. But, as I said, I didn't notice anything at first.

Spring came, then early summer: May, June. Other years she would have dwindled toward her seasonal somnambulence, but that year she didn't. She kept her ample, rolling roundness, and kept on singing happy sassy songs under the sun. Just kept right on moving, awake, and bright, and satisfied. Then I saw that she had spread herself into a pond.

I suspected it must be for you that she was opulent, so I went to look. Only a short walk downstream, just out of sight of the house, and-- of course--there you had built a monster show-off dam. What a guy! What a performance! A few yards further down where the banks come together, you could have made the same pool with a quarter the work. But no, you wanted to do it with a flourish, wanted to play a strutting extravagant game. Later, upstream past the studio, I found you had made two more dams for her to tumble over. No wonder she sang.

After that I looked for you at the pond. Glimpsed you occasionally, especially in the evenings, from kitchen door, or footbridge. Mostly I saw your nose moving across her rippling skin, pushing that wet wedge, nuzzling the voluptuous membrane where water meets air. Sometimes, at dusk, I watched you circle her, sniffing, patting, shaping, as an attentive and possessive lover does. Sometimes I was startled by your slapping, for no reason apparent to me. I guess that is another of your watery games: a kind of love-play with the wanton you adore.

I remember how delighted I was, before I was dismayed. It seemed an affluence to have both of you at my door-step: a new amplitude of water, and an unanticipated brother bundled in slick fur. But I saw how quickly you cleaned off the thicket of salmonberry and then of course you were looking for what next. I was surprised at your taste for cedar, and your disdain for alder, the opposite of what I would have predicted. (The book says alder ranks with willow as one of your favorites.) In a single night you made a path from pool-side to where I felled a maple for firewood; so I left the branches and bucked up the trunk to make it easy for you—so you could roll the short lengths to get at their underbellies—and then each morning I saw how you had been up in the night feasting.

Then I saw that you were moving on from little cedars to big cedars--all the cedars you could get your paws on--and not bringing them down either, just ringing them. "Hey"--I said--"what's that about?" You didn't answer, pretended not to hear me. I was conscious of the first intimations of disenchantment.

Next thing I knew you had been right up to my house and a thicket of elderberry and ocean spray was gone. Next night, a lovely mountain ash. Not long after that a small plum tree disappeared--nipped off and simply vanished--and then a blue-flowering ceanothus, by the studio. I heard by island telegraph that a beaver had been up on a neighbor's porch, peering in her window, just like the raccoons do in Toronto. At this point dismay gave way to the first hints of panic. How long till you figure out how to get through the deer fence into the garden? You are going to want our apple and pear trees! Do you also have a gourmet taste for raspberries? Currents? Honeysuckle? Delicate Japanese maples? I have heard that, like rabbits, you go for carrots, cabbage, beets. . . . I stood by the bridge and called to you. "Excuse me for disturbing you," I said, "but I think we need to have a little talk." Again you didn't answer. You didn't even show your face above the water.

We called up the local biologists for advice, but mostly what we got was their favorite horror stories about your exploits elsewhere. Like the guy who hooks up a 12-volt battery to a wire strung an inch above the water. Thinking, hard heart, to fry you as you swim. Surprise! He comes out next morning and finds that you have raised your pond just enough to short out his system.

The biologists explained why live-trapping and moving you beavers is not an effective solution. We were advised to try culverts through the dams, with intakes far enough upstream that you won't be able to figure out where your water is going. But the pipes we installed, with great effort, were too small to make any difference. I guess you had a laugh.

Then I got the idea of putting a hex on you. If I make a couple of life-size beaver effigies--and make them thoroughly demented--maybe they will protect the garden and ornamentals by a sort of scarecrow effect. An experiment in down-home voodoo. Maybe I can give you the shudders and you will start to think about moving on.

All of this didn't happen at once: it played out over two winters and summers.

We were hoping that you hadn't really meant to settle here after all. It was just a romantic fling wasn't it, not a forever thing? Or, at the very least, could you experience an epiphany please? Could you eat from now on only the cedars that you have already killed? (I reckoned they might last you about eight or ten years, finely chewed.)

For days at a time I tried not to think about you at all. But bushes kept disappearing.

I put my faith in the two new effigies of the evil eye. What else to do? (They look like they were sent out from central casting to the set of Beaver Space Aliens.)

I was terribly double-minded about you; loved having you about, and increasingly apprehensive about your intentions. I did not want a major war with you.

You were here a couple of years, with border skirmishes. You never did get into the garden. Maybe you listened to my plaintive protestations after all and just pretended not to. Maybe you knew that I really did love you. Anyhow, one evening late winter I was down at the beach not far from where your watery love pours herself over a rock ledge, under some hanging branches and huckleberries and out into the chuck. There you came lolliping out from under those bushes across driftwood and gravel, more or less toward me. At first I thought you were a giant otter of amazing corpulence. You moved, I thought, otterish, more quickly than I would have thought of beaver, with that rolling wavy movement that is so graceful and endearing in the otter family and, I see now, in yours.

"Is that you? Am I dreaming? If it is you, what are you up to?"

You looked right at me for a moment, then, to my astonishment made for the edge of the salt water, plunged in and headed off, perhaps toward the island a mile away. Or was it toward the mythical isle of silver willows, bending to catch their eternal reflections in golden ponds? I think I must have assumed, that evening, that you were just playing the eccentric, out for an ocean dip. But you never came back.

Did you know I was on the beach that evening? Coincidence, or did you choose the moment? Was it a generous-hearted goodbye? Are you indeed a prince, and were you granting me my wish?

It has been a year now, a bit more, without you. I miss you. The naiad misses you--I heard her murmuring your name. She made it through last summer, somewhat less exuberant than when you were here but not wasted. Living on memories I guess. Inclined to dreams and reminisces. Two of your dams are still intact, and she still sings as she moves over them, though with a certain note of melancholy. As for me, I never glance out of the kitchen window nor step out onto the back porch but my eyes turn to the pond, expecting to see that familiar vee moving across it.

I will not tear out your dams, nor drain your pond, even though the old leaning firs still have their feet in water. Some of those dead cedars will stand as snags for many years. Should be terrific for the Downys and Hairys and Pileated.

By the way, I really do not think it was me or my silly scare-beavers that spooked you. Probably you fussed about me much less than I did about you. Really, I think you live in a magical story. What you are is lavishly in love with water, ardent for big, wet adventures. This little splash wasn't enough to hold you but for a moment.

I imagine you a furry fir cone dreaming it fell into moving water, dreaming your transformation into a wander-lust beaver-prince, who dreams, even now, the deep swim of the dolphin, of the Orca, or perhaps the Great Blue.

Well, happy travels, whoever, wherever, you may be. You put your mark on the stream and on me. If you think about us, picture her much as you ponded her. And me? Glad for her company. Glad for your memory.

7. WATER

Come, walk down to the water with me. I want to show you something. I'll tell you as we go.

There will be seaweed drifts from the storm last night. We could take the wheelbarrows and gather some. But no, I'm not looking for seaweed this time. Not for driftwood either, though I suppose if there is a sculpted piece right in front of me and I can carry it perhaps I will.

What I'm looking for may be heavier, improbable to carry. What is it? It seems to be wet. Anyhow, I think I know where to start. There is a rock wall, a tapestry of green and sheen and shale: four or five mosses, and worts, and Narrow Beech Fern. A hanging garden, a little memory of Babylon, watered from some interior source. Come and see.

We won't go down by the usual path. This other way, a steep scramble to beach pebbles, to cabin-size boulders intimate together, so a body turning sideways can just slide between them.

Here. That little torrent at the fringe of huckleberries is the mouth of the stream where we were walking this morning, the stream who was loved by the beaver. Just up a few hundred yards from here we stood by his dam. Over there he set out to sea. See that rocky point--there is a smooth shelf that is terrific for sunbathing, and for diving off when a warm tide is in. It is also the best place for getting out into breakers and spray when there's a southeaster howling up the channel. But turn your back to the ocean--look at this little cliff face.

Water out of rock. Weeping, spilling, spurting. Has Moses been here, commanding it with his rod? Or is it a lesser predictable Nile, pouring from the ancient aquarian pitcher?

Regardless of prayers or petitioners, the wall is wailing. And in a heart of stone about four miles from here, somewhere deep in the ridge that is the long wave-length of the island, must be the valve of these tears.

Do I know these tears? They taste a familiar salt. I will go underground, seeking an earth sorrow. I will reach, extend, become liquid. Reach into rock, move in and up, through the finest veins and arteries, toward old, dark, all-but-forgotten sources, odorous of night. Up into something cavernous, into still blind space, perceptible only as emptiness. As if I were a mole probing darkness, sensing no resistance. A troll sits, silent, barely luminous, by an unseen ripple of water. Shadowy, shaggy, black-robed ancestors, bear and bison. Take me, brothers, to the spring of sorrows.

It is said that Raven brought the rivers of Haida Gwai one night; carried them in a single beak to the islands, from a mainland mountain. Brought them from that lofty, white-haired old fellow who offered to braid a dozen more before morning. Braid them from high splashed streamers of starshine, and the shape-shifting of cedar shadows.

It is said that by the slender source of any salmon stream sits a lovely maiden weaving water music--variations on renewal and return-- from silver desires and strands of her own dark hair.

It is said that we too are water--like lettuce and cucumbers and The Way. All juice: blood, ecstasies, rhythm and desire.

Impetuous sap sucks up from damp duff under us, sucks up through spun strands, up two hundred feet, three hundred, to pour through the eye of the little green skyward needle: elegant, alchemic laboratory, where the modest miracles of beauty and oxygen make me a rich man at heaven's gate.

Water leaping. Higher than forests, higher than clouds--cumulus, stratus, altostratus, cirrus--leaping beyond blue, out into the ice-bright furnace of space, to the edges, to that seed-center zero of original silence before the big drum roll. Every place, every interstice: space-wandering snowball comets, ice-crystal rings be-jewelling Saturn; ice-crusted moons dancing around Jupiter. Underdust frozen reservoirs deep in the pores of our own bright moon companion. Deep in space, in body, in mind. From the mother of mysteries, a colossal flinging out and gathering back, a tide calling. Certain uterine return.

Here on the edge of a continent her rains drench us. Here in the rain-forest she fills cups and boots to overflowing, penetrates, saturates, turns smart minds to ooze. Decrees epidemics of cabin-fever. Sponsors fly-aways, sun-seeking. But not for me. The exotic sun-spot posters do not call to me as clearly as my own damp acre does. Welcoming her wet hand against my window, I savor the season. I read, write, look to friendships, feel smug inventing hours in the greenhouse, go out to garden tasks between squalls. Check the rain-sheltered peach and apricot: are they happy? Prune the apples, raspberries, forsythia; prod the inhaling, exhaling earth. Gather flung fir tips, sap scents, a storm-scatter of profligate excess.

Another front moving over. We are sheltered here from gale-force winds, but there will be trees down somewhere on the island. Power out again? Come in close to wood heat. Light candles, remember how to cook on wood.

Firewood time. Take down the big leaning alder that's beginning to drop branches on the workshop. More juice, intensely orange, spills out from under pale pungent skin. Trim, buck, haul, split, stack: meditation for a week and comfort for a winter. This is labor for CEOs to covet, especially the splitting. Easy, voluptuous, rhythmic effort. Milk flesh; tangerine blood. An old communion, out of time, this yielding to the ax, this passionate surrender.

A sufficient little cosmos is encircled here, at the chopping block, in front of the wood shed.

A fragment of the original explosion echoes in this sweet sharp snap: muscular wood strands releasing their intimate embrace.

Rain spatters again.

Come in to the refuge of the pottery studio: bright and warm, with music for choosing, here is an irresistible opulence. In this womb-- sheltered, nurtured--the universe is an opportunity for endless messing about with mud. Wet mud, stiff mud. The wheel or the slab. Try modeling, that most primitive conversation between earth and water, a pair of hands, and a pointed stick.

Perhaps the oldest modeling of clay is in a vast cave known as Tuc d' Audoubert, in the French Pyrenees. It is a pair of bison, each two feet long. From a certain vantage point the male appears to be mounting the female. Deep inside a mountain, by crude lamp or torchlight, someone modeled beloved animals--a sister and a brother, a pair of power beasts-- from wet earth, modeled them in a most protected place, no doubt in a particularly holy place, where they might mate undisturbed, unseen but by the inner eye for a few millennia. For a good part of our lifetime, pictures of these two surviving bison have been in the art books, labeled "masterpiece." But the beasts themselves had been living under the mountain, forgotten and unknown, for sixteen thousand years. They are three or four times older than the Egyptian pyramids. I assume that Praxiteles, Michaelangelo, and Rodin heard no audible whispers of Tuc d' Audoubert, yet they dipped into the same pool that a nameless paleolithic sculptor drank from and dreamt into.

Nearby the two bison of Tuc d'Audoubert, in slightly wetter locations, are mounds of mud where companion sculptures have dissolved. Just a bit too much water, and images which endured, endured, endured... are erased in a moment.

No matter. The Zen master deliberately breaks the vessel. Apparently the treasure is not in the pot but in the emptiness which remains. One must assume that the water it held for a moment was content to be contained there only as a pause in the journey and now once more is on its way to the ocean.

Noah's great flood still moves toward the matrix.

Aphrodite's birth is from the ocean, a brief coalescence of sea-tossed foam. After the goddess has given us flowers and springtime, slippery pleasures and jealousy, I guess she returns to her salt-water source. Returns into herself.

But today I do not look out to the ocean. She is too deep for me. Today, rain is enough. Just now, this stream suffices, this spilling bank is plenitude.

If you come here on one of the coldest days of winter you will find the rock wall iced, and still weeping. Glistening draperies of ice points, strung beads, garlands, daggers dripping, a fanciful tracery of crystal light.

Come summer, there will be a wall of color. Tufts and cushions and streamers of moss: wine red, crimson, orange, and black, complimenting deep shiny greens, pale greens, olive, and golden greens. There will be pink primrose, white saxifrage, montia, and sandwort. There will be a cascade of yellows over the top of the cliff: buttercups, and monkey flowers. And blue periwinkles.

But today is storm season, cloud season. Colors are muted. Odors of damp vegetation seem to emanate from the rock itself. Out of fissures between rock layers come seeps and trickles, gathering into a small cascade. Today, all of them seem to be tears. Tears flowing to the sea, eager to be there. Let them go. Let them flow.

Of course I do not know whether the island is crying. And if she is would I know why?

If these were my tears I would be able to say something.

The forests of this island are being felled, as fast as the ferry can carry loaded trucks to the other side. Feeding a Cyclops: a monstrous one-eyed appetite, a heavy hammer.

The lake at the heart of the island is under ravage. Bite by massive bite, her watersheds are logged. Gouged for roads. Raked for house space. Silt and septic affluent foul this water that a only a few eyeblinks ago was clear as the sight of eagles. And more houses on the way. More septic fields. More of us.

More of us.

The age-old question of the sage:

Do you have the patience to wait
until your mud settles and the water is clear?
Can you remain unmoving
until the right action arises by itself?

May be a long wait.

Simple facts. Profound losses.

Rain continues to fall, on the forests, and on the memories of
forests.

8. BOUNDARIES

The summer I was eighteen my brother and I saddled up and rode south into the foothills of the Rockies.

We rode through valleys green-garmented in aspens, garlanded with silver streams. Rode across hillside meadows where herds of wild horses, flowing grass up to their bellies, snorted and galloped. Rode steep bluffs where long-fingered pinion pines, urged by an imaginative wind, twisted themselves into bonsai contortions. At treeline, we camped by a mountain lake--a "tarn" I suppose--perfectly round, perfectly clear, warmed by the summer sun, where we disturbed the perfect reflections of sky, cloud, and saskatoon scrub, with a late afternoon swim.

Next morning, the rest of the way was on foot. The last mile or so, to the base of the mountain, was jagged jumbled rock-fall, too dangerous for horses. Equipped only with a lariat, the blessing of a raven, and youthful innocence, we went up the awful sheer face of Old Chief Mountain, had intimate conversations with terror and ecstasy--punctuated by time-stop moments of total concentration on the next handhold-- survived, exulted, and came down again.

Found our horses.

Rode home.

Chief Mountain, bold skyline vista of my childhood, icon, talisman, was my first, and remained for half a century, my most potent experience of a power spot, a sacred space. Until I came here, to this spot of sometime sun, in a shade-cool forest.

It was decades ago that I last saw him, but Old Chief Mountain remains a powerful presence in memory's eye. He is one who demands and gets attention. His shape is striking, his setting dramatic. He is the subject of local stories, paintings, and millennial speculations. He is enveloped in the lore of the First Nations, his voice deeply resonant in tribal memory.

How, I ask myself, can an unassuming unknown almost hidden place, a mere opening in the woods, compare with a magnificent angular upthrust of stone which dominates a prairie skyline for a hundred miles? There is nothing even remotely so wonderful, so visibly and spiritually compelling, about a modest house in a small clearing, with courtyard and workshop, garden, and a few steps by a leafy path to a foot-bridge over a stream. Yet, as surely as I had it as a boy approaching the foot of the mountain, sacred space is the experience I have here.

Here.

This tapestry of many voices. Green voices. Liquid voices. I am nourished here, by the sweet, slender note of the Varied Thrush at dawn. I am pulled back here, if ever I should venture away, by a wind that hints of seaweed, cedar, and gardened earth. More than any cathedral, any mosque or tabernacle where I may have visited and worshipped, this physical acre contains all the sacred songs and rituals I feel a need to know. A physical ground--with beets, beans, and garlic--has more power in my imagination than the most fanciful visions of grace or glory might have had.

But now I am puzzling about edges. If this ordinary acre is a sacred space where does it leave off and the non-sacred, the profane, begin? How shall I know the moment when I cross over the boundary?

It seems easy enough to say where a mountain begins and ends. The edge of a clearing. The outset of an adventure. A magical sequence may be contained within a frame of convention: "Once upon a time. . . and they lived happily ever after."

"Sacred" may not be that easy.

This morning I walk down to the smell of salt, stand between driftwood and tide pools watching a cloud of Bonaparte's gulls dipping and diving. A heron waits, silhouette of eternity. Behind me, I am told, is a native burial spot, and petroglyphs hidden by undergrowth.

A half mile along the beach is a large cave, its entrance curtained by maples, where a few years ago otters played and nested. Otter spirits linger. Otter dreaming.

Further along, the rocky cliffs where eagles preside. Below, rock shelves where sea lions may still haul out to sunbathe, though now for the most part they rest on the islets further out.

Then there is the hidden valley where a stream bank is unmarked by paths, where the trees are so old, the moss and silence so deep, that it is possible to brush against the boundary of primeval memory: a delicate spider-web sensation against the brain. Nothing clearly in focus, but teasing glimpses, hints of first wonder-moments, of elder beings, pointy eared and furry. There... a shadow at the edge....

From this valley, walk up the ridge to the cleft-rock heart of the island, where bats live in deep fissures which few humans would care to enter. And if we did venture in, would a homely oracle speak? Would she be as bending as Delphi's to our minds?

Come down by the lake, where swans and geese are the most imposing of at least a dozen resident waterfowl, follow the creek toward the sea, and home again, from a walking tour that could have filled a leisurely day, or a half day. A walk that dry-brushed the homes of twenty or thirty human neighbors, venturing, at most, perhaps five or six miles from my kitchen door. And all of it--every step and stone--is spirit-home. All shot with the divine: no shadow where the gods are not. So, if I am to discover non-sacred space, I must look further afield.

* * *

You will see that I am not very interested in the boundaries of property or ownership, the ones marked by high fences and stout walls. The Romans were interested in those, and they set their god Terminus to guard them, to make them solid. But long before him was that quicksilver spirit, primordial Hermes, the one who moved like air or mischief from one dimension to another. Moved through fluid boundaries, more like membranes than palings. Perhaps the sacred is like that. Elusive at the edges. Liable to leak out from any container.

Would you expect sacred space to be the known or the unknown? For me, it seems, intimacy reveals it. In some cases, at any rate, power *becomes*: the more mysterious, the more alive, as it is lived with. About a hundred and fifty years ago a New Englander is said to have remarked "I have traveled much in Concord." He liked traveling by foot, and reckoned that one may know as much of the world as he can walk: say, for example, a twenty mile radius from home. In his case home was for a season a hut by Walden Pond.

A grizzly bear, it is said, requires a home range, undisturbed by humans, of at least a similar radius. And grizzlies are great walkers. If removed from their range upwards of a hundred miles, they can be quickly home again. In certain respects their intimacy with home would appear to be many times ours. It is thought that grizzlies hear and see about as well as we do, but for deep knowing of their world they use their noses. Aboriginal people have said: When a leaf falls in the forest, the eagle sees it fall, the deer hears it fall, and the grizzly smells it fall.

There is a somewhat permeable boundary around any world I can know. Might I have walked and canoed across the continent with an Alexander Mackenzie or a David Thompson, the whole distance would have been, in a sense, known to me: at least the corridor I traveled. But I think no transplanted European has known, nor ever can know, this land as the people knew it to whom it was ancestral home. The grizzly-monster that the pale man transmogrified was not the grizzly-brother the darker man had smoked the pipe with.

Europeans crossed the physical boundary of the Atlantic and at the same time moved through a more challenging cultural boundary, a boundary of imagination, into a space which they called "wilderness." Of course it was not any such thing to its native inhabitants.

Long before journeying to the Americas, Europeans had become attached to their distinction between wild and civilized. They still had places called wild in the old countries, and they had moved far enough away from them to become fearful and dark and superstitious about their own places of origin. Access to these realms as *home* had been largely lost. So the boundaries of the wild came to be guarded by the beings of transformation and dark knowledge: the witch, the hermit, the serpent, all permutations of the Hermes figure. And Europeans, by and large, wanted them tamed too.

Aboriginal Americans did not, so far as I can tell, make a distinction between civilized places and wilderness, still less think to tame the wild. Until we brought them our Enlightenment I guess they remained at home and, for the most part, at ease, in the whole magnificent landscape of a continent. An at-homeness perhaps closer to the bear's than we who have removed ourselves can imagine. Nevertheless, they would have acknowledged that there is a danger as well as a teaching at certain edges, at important boundary crossings. And they too had their messenger-transformer beings to assist at these points of crossing over, for the edges that most compel us have an uneasiness woven into them. A hint of loss. Or of fearful transformation.

From a crossing over, one might never come back.

When the Haida sent Raven back to the beginning of the world, or to under-sea adventures, they used him as a proxy, to explore and to facilitate exchanges with the beings of these ultimately unknowable and inherently dangerous realms. No doubt people sometimes, in trance state, accompanied Raven on such journeys. And to his home in the air also, even to the place above the sky. To the several boundaries of "first things."

Meanwhile there was, and still is, the mischievous, mocking, garrulous black fellow who walks the same this-world beach as we do.

When is was time to re-tell a Raven story the time and place would be dignified, the language set apart with a special resonance, to signify and to honor the crossing over into the other realm. I would hesitate to call it the "sacred" realm. Gods, temples, and a big distinction between sacred and profane are part of the baggage we brought with us from Europe. The people native to these lands knew the powers and spirits of their place, but perhaps not "gods" in our familiar sense. Their approximations to European temples might be landforms of special concentrated potency: Old Chief Mountain, for example. Their experiences in some way paralleling our "sacred" might include dialogue with the animal teachers, or opening the ears to songs which forests and rocks are singing.

It looks like native spirituality has much to do with special attentiveness at boundaries, important courtesies observed there. Cultivation of the energy exchanges between human and non-human beings. Bears, for example. I am thinking of the hundreds, perhaps thousands, of variations on the story of the woman who marries into the bear clan. I notice in these stories the gifts received by humans from the bear. I try to imagine what the return gifts might look like, gifts from humans to the bear, which might complete a circle, re-create a balance.

A Tlinget native, wanting to travel or gather food in bear territory might address the bear with an honorific title. "Grandfather," he might say, "I am a human. I would like to trespass on your land today. I have not come to bother you, and I am not looking for trouble. You go your way, and I'll go mine." Something to that effect.

I have had only a few brief conversations-in-passing with bears, but, in earlier parts of my life I had plenty of opportunity for communion with farm animals. Horses, harnessed to pull things, with their amazing power, their humor, their patience with my idiosyncrasies. Milk cows, their dignity, their qualities of nurture. These beasts were amazingly courteous in their dealings with me. Occasionally the trickster appeared, to keep me alert. I had the experiences of being swatted, stepped on, bitten, dismissed, brushed off. But it was far more often me than they who failed in courtesy.

These days, the most compelling physical edge for me is the edge of the ocean. Relationship here is not easy. I hear the Mother calling, and sometimes I do not want to answer. My first time in the Pacific surf, many years ago, I was quickly pulled beyond my depth, began to drown, was astonished to find myself touching sand again, staggering and retching up the beach, until I could collapse on the sand just beyond her reaching fingers. Today, paddling my kayak--elegant featherweight membrane between breath and drowning--is always to some degree a conscious conversation with fear.

If there is a boundary more fearful than that of deep water, it must be the moment of death itself, the physical and the more-than-physical experience. The wise ones have said: Cultivate death as friend and advisor. A hard saying. One day, with luck, I will know the practice of a conscious dying, a spirited dying. I can even imagine the possibility of a kind of gladness and resonance with my own mortal decay. Meanwhile, of course, I am not glad at all. Age is creeping through my body, and I am experiencing the deer staring into the pit lamp.

I have attended at the awesome boundary of birth. Births of calves and foals, of lambs and kids. Births of human children, a couple of them quickened by my own seed. The gateway, the strenuous entrance, where I was dumb, and they shouted.

I have been pushed, or pulled, or simply tumbled, over trance edges into outrageous alternative geographies: lush fruitbowl provinces, sensuous undulating mountain ranges of melody.

A few times, I have been quiet enough to hear the loon, calling at the edge of time.

I have been to the boundary of love, skin on skin, and reached over.

The Ojibwa word *Manitou* is commonly translated "Great Spirit", but a better translation might be "something mysterious." It is this something mysterious which we encounter at boundaries, which, if we are not too skittish, or pompous, may facilitate our discourse with the beings of the other side.

On ancient maps, where known territory shaded off into the unknown, was found the admonition "Here be Dragons."

* * *

Most times, my attention is caught by *physical* edges. The edge of deep water, or of a brother being: his feather, his skin. Even death, and sacred space, for all their permeable edges, have tangible dimension. But there is a metaphysical boundary which puzzles me, and perhaps it is the most mysterious of all. It is the boundary of something unspeakable, where people tongue-stumble over "thus-ness," or "the void," or an unsettling metaphor:

> The blind students
> follow the blind teacher
> listening to the wisdom
> of the canes tapping.

It is said that on the other side of doing is "not doing." Watching? Perhaps. But not *doing*.

Aside from our clever ingenious astonishing juggernaut: the watching.

I grasp enough of the distinction to understand that I am an addict on the "doing" side. From the beginning of irrigation, and tamed wheat, some ten, twelve millennia ago, I have been an eager agent of all this exciting yang energy: getting and spending and laying waste. But recently I am noticing that something in me wants to rein in the big-foot beast I am riding. The me-beast seems to be trampling too many others. Today, I find myself wanting to set right what I see that I have been setting awry.

Me, the one with the teeth that are chewing up ancient forests like soft berries.

Me, the hundred-handed, whose long arm reaches down to rake the bottom of the sea.

Bulimic me, the one whom you see bulging, and who must keep on feeding the limitless belly.

Nauseated at last by my excessive doing, I imagine I want to *do* something about it. Me, the blind student, the dark joke, still harnessed to doing.

The voice of an ancient one, the pale and ghostly one, inside the big spruce: Greetings to you grizzly and to you salmon, to you eater, and you eaten. Greetings to you, the one who tramples.

So, is it true, as has been whispered, that there is another energy, an energy of the old earth, which is a turning season, yielding as water?

The sage has said: Practice not-doing, and everything will fall into place.

What would it be like to watch without trying to correct? What would it be like to sit in the back of the spruce with Grandfather and enjoy the show? I guess that means the whole show, even the gobbling beast with the huge teeth. Even me.

Barely, vaguely, dimly--again the brush of that fine spun web against my brain--I imagine the practice of rock. The practice of a still pool.

When we went up the mountain, our bodies were young and physical and glowing. They exulted in the rhythm of the horses, the silk of sun-warmed water, the reach and exertion and menace of the climb. Our senses were exuberantly awake. Our sense of privilege was sufficiently tuned that we sought permission. And it was granted.

We conquered no one; achieved nothing.

We left the Chief as we encountered him: enduring, rooted, implacable. We went to our limit, or, at least within glimpse of it, and there was no doing. Then we went home.

Somewhere, in the scrapbook that remains to me of that day on the mountain, I am looking for the yielding boundary which I suppose I am up against.

The voice of the old one: Observe the courtesies of every moon.

The voice of the sage: Do your work, then step back.

9. ROCK

You will find me outside the kitchen door. Out through the mudroom (a fine disarray of coats and boots), sitting on the back step, facing sun-up. The sun has reached out a long horizontal arm to brush me with the pale rose and gold of an artist's morning. No, that is a conceit. The sun came seeking the stone door-step, found it, and drenched it with impressionist light. Then I came out to try to claim a place in it, wanting to be in the picture.

Bright morning, too early to be warm. My favorite coffee cup warms my hands. A half dozen--maybe a dozen--different kinds of birds are singing. Singing their territories or their tasks, perhaps their loves, perhaps their springing joy. I am sitting on the step, listening to my world sing.

This flat-topped boulder on which I am sitting usually appears gray but just now, up close and light-bathed, it is white and black speckled, pebbly surfaced. Look closely: minute specks of silver are flashing amongst the white and black. Three parallel bands of creamier white divide the rock on a dramatic diagonal. At one edge there are four parallel gouges which make me think (however illogically) of a giant ice-age bear sharpening his claws on stone.

This door-step, of which I am un-accountably fond, is a chunk of granite deposited at this spot by a well-muscled back-hoe at the time when the foundations of the house were laid. It is a kind of cornerstone. Maybe it remembers the morning it came here some years ago, an early spring day very like today: the short journey from a hillside a mile or so north; being placed here, precisely, where a door would be. And perhaps also it brought with it earlier memories of longer and more strenuous journeys, shoved and carried by ice long before my kind were here to remark on it.

I am tempted to say--though this too would be a conceit--that a stone journeyed to me. Journeyed, long since, to this island, then sat through many seasons of sun and shade, waiting for me.

Whatever the imaginative fancy of the stone's journey to me it is true enough that over the years I have journeyed to stones.

* * *

I was nine years old when my parents took me from the prairie--where an up-thrust block-shaped mountain had been a beckoning mirage on the skyline--to the foothills, where that same mountain presided as undisputed Chief of the territory over which he looked. I was in my teens when I went up and touched him, and heard him tumbling down, and first knew the fragility of rock.

* * *

I was perhaps twenty when I went to Stonehenge. It was a bleak day, gray and chill. No one else was about. In those days, there were no fences, no ticket booths or concession stands, no marketing. Only a distant speckle of sheep...and wind over the cropped grass. I no longer remember what I expected, nor if I had any expectations. I remember that these stones on standing stones appeared unremarkable, trivial even, from far away across low empty hills. And then suddenly, up close, they took me with the quiet authority of a conflagration, filling completely the frame of my attention. Moved inside, filled my chest, belly, whole body.

Monolithic stones took the whole space of my consciousness so that for I don't know how long there was nothing else. They alluded to history of course, or to pre-history. To pre-memory. They spoke of nothing directly: mostly hints, rumbling silences, my own breath and heartbeat. They gave nothing away. They did not act mysterious or self-important, just self-contained. They were the purest, surest distillation of mystery and power I had until then encountered.

* * *

At twenty-one I climbed and wandered alone on the slopes of Mt. Blanc, above the steep villages and the even steeper hand-harvested hay fields, above the treeline in the sharp thinning air where bells of un-seen sheep at summer pasture sent clear tones leaping like silver from stone to stone.

* * *

I remember, a year or so later, a hot summer approach to Chartres, slowly, by bicycle, by a straight road between flat gilded fields of shimmering grain. Re-playing the memory, I see again cathedral spires rising--hazy, hovering, phantom-like over sheets of gold--then growing solid, and at last the buttressed delicate bulk of her, dominating the plains, magisterial as a mountain. I loved the a-symmetry of those not-quite-twin towers, the way they spiked me, disturbed me, spoke of defect, of off-balance, brought me back, still bring me back, as no perfectly matched pair ever could. I loved the lofty shadowed cavern of her interior, her hushed, high-arched belly. I went on--other years, other journeys--to other gothic cathedrals, but it was at Chartres that the eternal erotic first revealed herself to me in a metaphor of sacred stone. It was at Chartres that when the immense doors were opened, so were the eyes of my imagination.

* * *

Years later, I went with my love to the fragments which yet remain of the peacefully off-beat temple city of Paestum. It was early Italian spring. A passion of wild flowers had been flung by a careless giant across untended grass, sloping down from fine standing ruins. Whatever hustle of tourism and traffic there had been outside the gates receded, then disappeared, leaving the eloquent silence of stones. Silent stones rose up to meet us. Graceful un-roofed columns of rosy limestone, glowing in the Mediterranean light, opening up to luminous blue space. Birds tended to nests and to food. Insects buzzed, hummed, and droned. We surrendered to the sun-warmed day, and one by one the temples took us into their serenities.

Athena's.

Poseidon's

Hera's. The Mother Goddess. These fifty columns, an admirer suggests, are a choir to her honor. Singing stones. Enduring hymns of praise, in the afternoon.

* * *

Here, this early hour, on the rough stone step at my kitchen door, it is not afternoon, nor even warm. The brightness of the morning brought me out. It is just past spring equinox, so daylight is a few minutes longer than night. This is the first morning I am tempted out with my coffee. Looking east, I have glimpses of ocean through the trees. The sun is well up now, but still low enough to sparkle on the water, blinding me, so I have to look away. Nearer, this side of the trees, and winding into them, the stream and pond, mostly still in shadow. A pair of mallards feeding quietly, dabbling, the male occasionally flashing royal iridescent when he swims through a luminous streamer. Skunk cabbages hanging back in deep shade, but they will shout their butter yellow as soon as the painterly sun comes around to brush them with light.

Deer have been moving by the pond every morning about this time in groups of two, three, five: some looking coat-scruffy with spring molt, but all well fed. Yesterday I watched a doe lower her head to drink....

Spring growth of everything is lush: vanilla leaf, wild geranium, a few trillium, nettles. Several pairs of swallows were flying early acrobatics over the garden yesterday.

To my right, the compost and sea-weed boxes, and beside them, the sunlit path to my parents' house. Dad and Mother live just next door, beyond that screen of trees. Theirs is the path I take nearly every day. Not a long walk: dawdling it could take three or four minutes, in a hurry, only one. I go to their house to touch something solid. Something foundational. So far as I can tell, Dad and Mother have always been there. I try to imagine a day when they will not be there, and the picture won't focus. I feel shaky. There is the little-boy part of me afraid that the world will be too much for me without them. That I will lose my bearings, or my footing.

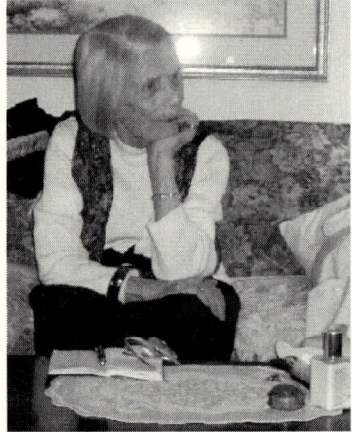

Dad is pebbly granite, the same texture and rugged outline as the stone I am sitting on. I go to him when something needs a fix: a motor, or a pair of shoes. His garden is large, and well tended.

Mother is fine-grained and smooth, for a lifetime has been polishing herself to a lustrous sheen. Jade, I think. I sit with dirt-stained trousers on her brocaded chair, and we tell each other the day's little stories. She offers me a chocolate, or a glass of liqueur in fine crystal.

Someone else might find them frail, more like reeds than rocks. Both are shrunken and bent and they move slowly, taking care. They lie down for afternoon naps. That is the presentation their bodies are making these days.

When I go to them it is to a place where eyes have remained alert through seasons of poverty and prosperity. I see courage, well weathered. I see where work and stamina have sculpted whole landscapes of valley and crag against these geologies of bones. I recall that day when my strong and vigorous father turned forty, and I felt fearful because he was growing old, that I might not have him much longer. That would be something like fifty years ago now. The next day, we were working in the forest and a branch gouged his eye, and I feared Dad would be blinded. Today he reads more easily than I do.

As I said, the fragile child in me persists. But so also does the one who takes courage from the rock under his hand.

* * *

Today I do not need a journey across a continent to seek conversation with a mountain or to sit by a temple of stone. Out Dad and Mother's driveway if I turn right there is a steep climb for a mile or so and a ridge-top, logged, bare to its bone in places, with views to ocean in both directions. Then, if you know where to look for it, a shadowed path little marked by human feet.

The forest floor begins to heave and buckle. Footing can be uncertain and dangerous, especially where there is undergrowth. Vertical crevices are wide enough for a foot or a body to slip into, so watch your step. Everything is deeply silent here, silent and shaded. It will be cool even in August. Northeast slope; plenty of moisture. Trees are large, many of them gnarly. Beards of moss hang from long gray chins. Underfoot beneath an overlay of green is a jumble of huge rock chunks, big as houses, big as ships. Trees find pockets to root in, then work patiently at making soil.

An ancient big-leaf maple at the edge of a cliff is perhaps the most complex I have ever seen, with huge horizontal trunks reaching out over another forest below. The curve of one of them, like a hammock, invites a pause and a rest. Go ahead: sit, and enjoy. The presence of this fine old grandmother is so embracing that I suppose anyone would want to stop and be held, for a childhood moment.

We are walking over that darkly resonating interior organ of our island which we refer to as "the caves." To find the caves, we leave the big maple and scramble down, around even larger heaved boulders, into thirty or forty-foot winding canyons, seeking narrow fissures which drop into darkness: I don't know how far. The earth has split, has broken; I guess she is still slowly breaking.

How many islanders have been here? Few, I think. Fewer in body than in imagination, for many of us will have heard of this place, without knowing quite how to find it. It will be spoken of more frequently in coming months, in coming days, spoken of in sorrow and dismay, for the chain saws and skidders are getting closer.

I remember the first time I came here and sat a long while, opening to the silence, thinking "here is the heart of the island"...listening for the heartbeat.

It is said that the heart of a certain mountain beats but once a year, and that it will be a cold night, just before dawn.

It is said that a climber will hear the voice of the mountain, will have conversations with the mountain, especially about immediate things, like gravity, and wings. Anywhere, everywhere, one must imagine mute rocks lack only a listener, to speak.

I sit on a massive mossy edge, above a small canyon, and ask about earlier times, before Europeans came. I know there were native settlements and camps along the shores of this island but what about here, in the heart of it? It feels as if anyone who comes here must be aware of stepping into a pool of concentrated up-welling energies.

"Did they come here?" I ask. "I mean right here, to this cleft in your body?" The maples, the cedars, lean imperceptibly forward to hear an answer. A pause, then:

Yes, they came here. They knew the secret-heart places as intimately as you are likely to.

"Did they have ceremonies here?"

No.

"What did they do here?"

They sat.

"Just that?"

They sat in the silence and listened. Like you.

I reach out a hand to touch the rock wall beside me. It is deeply furred, as a great quiet beast, furred with resilient green, vigorous, slightly damp.

I sit, and listen.

The stillness moves, moves like a smooth swell, from a dark wind, from a distant shore. A scrap of birch is carried on the swells. Through a silence that reaches back four centuries, eastward to the shores of Lake Ontario, I hear the voice of the one called "Peacemaker," speaking to the assembled chiefs of the Five Nations.

Think not, O Chiefs, of your own generation
but of continuing generations.
Think of those yet unborn, whose faces
are coming from beneath the ground.

It is said that the Peacemaker was a luminous figure who paddled
a canoe of white stone, a sign that the creator had sent him. It is said that
he planted a peace-tree and invited all tribes to sit under it. And that the
confederation he called for, based on negotiation rather than on prowess,
lasted for ten generations.

I reach out a hand, as if to touch the generation moving on,
ahead of me. There is my father, bending over his beans and his corn.

I reach back toward the generation coming after me. I am the
father now, an astonishing notion! I try to grasp it, to make it real, but it
slips away. Shall I, insubstantial as time, be a standing stone for my son,
for my daughters, as Dad has been for me? Is it possible that already I am
an icon for them: even now?

Questions to make me smile. If, like the stony ramparts of Old
Chief Mountain, I appear obdurate, the truth is that year by year, moment
by moment, he and I are tumbling down. That, I suppose, is as it should
be. Don't make the mountain too solid. Leave spaces for the faces
beneath the ground.

If I were able, I would leave them these stones, this peace, un-
trampled.

Were such gifts mine to give, I would leave to them the quiet
songs of all the un-roofed temples, the companionship of all mosses, and
clean lively water for their kayaks.

Older than the Peacemaker's white canoe, older than Chartres, or
Hera's columns, or Stonehenge--who knows how many generations
older?--the enduring one sees through them all, looks through the light of
ten thousand rising suns, and the pale light of ten thousand lowering suns,
sees me sitting here on my doorstep, and solemnly winks.

In complete stillness
a stone girl
is dancing.

10. DEER

Deer, I am thinking, can be such elusive fanciful beings. Onto whatever screens we gazed before rice-paper deer must have been etched, a very long time ago, etched and brushed in ochre, with the same delicate evocative lines we look for in old faded Chinese water colors and ink drawings.

In a big book I have seen deer drawings on pottery from the Neolithic, vigorously and confidently incised, and the conception is so light that the creatures fly. They seem to be studies in pure abstracted energy. They whirl and swirl like spinning tops. Like little cyclones, like dervishes. They combine deer with water and serpent motifs--anyhow that is what the archaeologist says. I might have just seen mandalas in motion. Who can tell where antler becomes wave becomes coil?

It seems clear enough that these are not representations of someone's favorite food source. They seem to be more about stepping

out into the oldest dance.

Where I live deer energy is not quite so esoteric but still, on any particular day, these powerful and graceful beings may dance in and out of the picture in a disconcerting way. They are all around us, often in plain sight, sometimes a rustle, a glimpse, a whisper. They appear and disappear as they will, like smoke, or like teasing half-remembered phrases in stories from childhood. When they are gone a quivering lingers in the dappled light.

Let me tell you about a rather odd encounter I had not long ago.

It was a late fall day, slanting rain, blustery and cold out. I was taking it easy inside, sitting in my favorite chair, with the murmuring warmth of the fire and the body heat of my old tortoise-shell cat, snoozing on my lap. She is named Kabira, this cat, from the Persian poet, Kabir. Years ago when she came to stay with me for a sabbatical summer she would quote some of his lines, such as these:

> Friend, hope for the Guest while you are alive...
> it is the intensity of the longing for the Guest
> that does all the work....
> Don't let a chance like this go by!

I resisted this poetic cat but she wore me down. So, in the end, she stayed on and has lived with me now more than a dozen years, and is getting arthritic and clumsy, and every year more crotchety. Anyhow, on this particular day she was making soft little mewing sounds in my lap, as if her dreams were kittenish, and this was a pleasant change from the mostly strident demanding petulant sounds that come out of her mouth these days.

So, there I was, just sitting, enjoying the sounds of fire and cat and rain.

There was movement at the front door. It is a glass door and I was startled to see a soft black nose pressed right up against it. Someone was looking in and--I had the impression--wanting to come in. No audible request. No doorbell or knocking. Just that steady looking in, and then the head turned and she caught my eye. I thought, "No, that *isn't* a deer at my door, asking to come in!" Then I thought, "Well, it *is* a miserable wet day out there; who wouldn't want to come in by the fire?"

I went to the door and opened it and said "Hello" and then, "Come in" and ... now what do I say? It was so unexpected, and at the same time oddly ordinary. I felt disoriented, that's for sure, but then a gladness came up, an old familiarity, and suddenly I wanted to hug, as if it were a just remembered family thing, but of course I stood there like a goof. It was like those embarrassing times when one person reaches out to shake hands and the other reaches out to hug and eventually you do both, with a little awkward dance at the arms and shoulders. Except this time no one shook hands *or* hugged, just that little shuffle of emotions.

Then my mother's manners kicked in, and I said "Would you like to sit down?" and "Would you like a cup of tea? Real, or herbal? Milk? Sugar?" And I guess she must have said "yes," because the next thing I knew I was putting the kettle on.

When I brought the tea my visitor had sat herself on the sofa, and she balanced the cup just fine so I relaxed a bit. She snorted quietly when she went to taste it, then waited for it to cool, and before long she was sipping politely.

Of course Kabira had waked when I set her off my lap, and now she was asking for tea, which was really very unusual. I tell you in all these years she has *never* asked for tea before. I found a very small cup for her, and when I handed it to her she surprised me again by saying "thanks". Then she insisted on getting back onto my lap and I was *sure* this was going to end in disaster with hot tea spilled on me--I already mentioned how stiff and clumsy Kabira has been getting lately.

Well, finally everybody was settled, and I could take time to look at my guest. I thought: she is an *old* doe, she has seen a lot of seasons. What made me think that, gave me that impression of maturity? She was plump enough and healthy looking, with a sleek coat of beautiful earth colors, mostly shades of sienna, with white at the throat and belly, white ear fringes, and some black trimming too. Her nose, as I said before, was shiny black, and so were her large expressive eyes, or very dark brown at any rate, and now I saw that her eyes were set off by long dark lashes handsome as a girl's.

I heard myself asking "How are your kids doing?" And then my internal dialogue: *that* wasn't right; you should have asked "How are your *children*?" or "How are your *fawns*?" Somehow I was pretty sure that this was the mother I had seen all summer with two yearlings *and* two little ones still in their spots.

I'm not sure what she answered: something about the older ones getting involved in their first romances, and, I think, some minor discipline problems with the younger ones. I'm afraid I was only half listening. My mind had skipped over to gardens and I was wanting to ask her why we can't ever be sure what deer are or aren't going to eat-- rhododendrons, for instance--why is it that for years the rhodos seem safe, with deer wandering by all the time, and then one day you look over and one is getting munched right before your eyes? And why we can go for years with deer regularly patrolling outside the netted garden, and then one morning they have been in and out again, and the strawberries and the peach are decimated, and it's like spirits have ghosted in and ghosted out, and no one can tell where or how.

I was feeling all at the same time rather stern and censorious and whiny about this, and wondering if I was going to get right into it with this beautiful creature, and knowing it would be right over the line into rudeness.

She, meanwhile, had got on to El Nino, remarking on the mildness of last winter and wondering how this one would be, and asking me if I had heard about the tropical fish that had apparently been seen up here in these northern waters.

Before I could answer about the fish she said smiling, "Well, look who's here!" and I saw she was looking at the window behind me so I turned and looked and there were the faces of the five young bucks I had seen hanging around together, off and on, this season: the oldest one, three-pronged; the youngest one just spiked; and a pair of the in-between ones that I had noticed before were well matched in size and adolescent energy. I was pretty sure they were the pair I had seen many times through the summer, playing rowdy tag through the forest, back and forth, banging and thumping with huge bounds careless of how much racket they made. I had looked at them through the poet's eye, and heard his voice:

... as if each leg were a gun
loaded with leaps ....

Then I was remembering the petite pair of spotted fawns that for a while in August hung around the pottery courtyard. I was remembering how they had come right over to see what I was making, and how when I had asked, "Where's your mom?" they had tossed their pretty heads as if they didn't need her anymore because they were feeling quite grown up now and quite brave and curious about everything all on their own. I laughed when they looked longingly at the pansy baskets hanging over their heads, as if by looking so enchanting and delicious they could charm me into lowering those flower feasts down to mouth level. Ha! Some chance!

By this time my visitor, the old doe, was chuckling at what she was seeing, and following her eyes from window to window I wondered if the whole forest was coming to look in on our tea party. I thought I glimpsed beaver for a moment at one window before eagle shoved in front of him looking pompous and silly with fish scales stuck to his beak. I saw frog and slug at another window and a pointed spear-shadow behind them, and before I could cry a warning, they were snapped up and gone.

There was only a cedar branch tap-tapping on the window and behind the branch dark night, and a glimpse of moon. Then cedar and moon faded out behind what I realized was a curtain of snow. And there, for a hammered iron moment, was raven: black as time, snow dusted, beckoning me out into the storm, beckoning me with an imperious unblinking eye that saw my resistance and pulled me right out through it.

I do not remember how I got outside--whether I dressed for the blizzard, whether I said goodbye to the doe or to Kabira--I was out in a scrubby forest. Not the towering shelter of our big firs and cedars but northern twisted smallish trees, with wind howling through them, pellety snow whipping over them.

Looming up in front of me now in the boreal night is the Reindeer Mother, great mother of northern peoples, huge and grand and powerful, larger than a moose, shaggy, her head lifted by a glorious air-borne sweep of antlers. I see that I am furred by a Laplander's parka, as warmly furred as the Deer-Mother, and fur-booted too, and we are running through the night, hoofs pounding, boots slapping, through an emptiness of ice, lit with high jagged pulses of electric color, and I am as warm as she, and I can run as fast as she, and the rush over frozen waste is intoxicating. I feel we might run to eternity, might run out over an edge into the swirl of flashing sky.

Now, as if I have won my hooves, I am as four-footed as she, and I too wear a flight of antlers. Now the odors of fur and animal heat are glorious to me. I am surrounded by a herd, I am running with my herd, hundreds of us, perhaps thousands, thunder under our hooves, ecstasy flaring in our nostrils.

The night thunders.

Space thunders.

Ice screams and cracks.

The Reindeer Mother is panting and heaving. She is birthing our world--our beginning--in fire and ice. A lusty leaping globe, crystal and sparking, is straining to be out of her. I must catch it in my hands. I can do this thing. I reach for it.

Fire flames out from the rim of this new-born nature. Glowing liquid rock is contracting to solid. Ice, in massive sheets, bunches and shoves, hesitates, retreats. An ice-world melts and gathers into a clear pool, under a bright fountain.

In her pool the Deer Mother bathes--fur gone, only an aura of antler remaining, body rounded now and rose tinted--here she bathes, with attendant nymphs, reveling and cavorting. We are all in the pool--me too--an exquisite seduction of cool water under a transparent Aegean sky.

Is it immodest for me to be here, savoring so much succulent female sensuality?

She hears my thoughts, and, in a mischievous gesture, splashes me.

I sense my own body growing succulent. I run my hands over it. Sleek skin, swelling belly and breasts, only a patch of fur. I look down at myself. I too seem to be woman. My belly moves under my hands as if it, also, would birth a world. I bask. I glory. But there is the excited yapping of hounds drilling my ears, exploding a reverie. Suddenly shot with terror I am scrambling from the pool, bounding, crashing, heedless, in panting leaps through the forest, blinded by fear. The physical terror of loosed dogs. The soul terror of finding myself suddenly again furred, and four-footed, again antlered. Finding myself stag. Knowing myself prey.

I hear the arrow whisper before I feel its rip, an opening at the heart, and liquid life draining out of me. I am on the forest floor, face flat against duff and twigs. Looking down at myself, sprawled, I see the dark pool widening out from me. Looking up from wet litter single-eyed, I meet the eyes of the archer bending over me; the one already receding into a blurred distance; the smooth-faced innocent un-formed one; the face so like a familiar photo, in an album, in the drawer.

Now the one bending--tending--over me, is the Lady of the Wild Things. She has shushed the excited hounds. They grow still, they root, they put on the green sleeves of saplings.

With hands of doves she lays me beside her clear pool. Washes me. Draws me down with her, held by her, into sweet water. I am under the water and she is under the water. I see her undulating, flickering as a fish. I see myself flicker. Sun through the water is glittering and glinting across our bodies. She is slow silver, moving as brilliant liquid, and she wraps her silver strands around me.

The one who wraps herself around me is the silver serpent and I am the ebony serpent and we are the ancient coiling ones. We are the awakening and the great sleep. We are the pushing out and the gathering in. We wrap ourselves, nine coils, around a crystal sparking globe. And the turning world grows still while we writhe and turn.

The world is a still stone head, smooth, immense, her blank carved eyes inward seeing. This great bleached oblivious face weathers, erodes, cracks... and storms move over her, desert caravans rest in her shadow and move on... nights fall, seasons turn, and still the serpents writhe and coil at her pale brow, and still her eye is inner.

The creases around her eyes have deepened into crevices. A fine line of light shines out of a fissure into dark and rain. I slide into a crevice in cool wet stone, put my eye to a crack of light, and try to focus on the interior scene.

Through the crack I see well enough the portion I can see. In there appears to be a simple comfortable room. The warmth of a wood fire, an elderly cat dozing in front of it. In an easy chair, enjoying a cup of tea, sits an elegant doe.

There is a tap-tap at an unseen door, and the doe rises to welcome her guest.

11. CEDAR

While still a young man, I brought my young family to live on this northwest coast. I wanted them to know farm rhythms and farm animals. I wanted them to know ocean tides, and the great forests. Very quickly, I bumped up against my contradictions.

Looking for land to farm, in a farming community, I was taken to a remnant parcel--a hundred acres or so--of undisturbed old forest. Very old forest. That day, that hour, decades ago, I experienced forest majesty.

A bright day, early summer. I remember the abrupt transition from a familiar spread-out world, drenched in transparent light, into an exotic enclosed world, suffused with shades of translucent green, layered and laminated of gently luminous airs, thick, tangible with motes, and breathing.

A sense of being seen, surrounded by great watching eyes. And yet, immersed in a kind of detachment too, watching turned inward, to private and protracted contemplation.

I remember, of course, stepping from hot into cool.

I remember a rising up of aromas, the piquant mixed pungencies of growing and decaying.

Most of all, I was confronted by the transition from an ordered world into an enormous and fantastic jumble, into tangle, and riot.

Leave the road, where cars go.

Leave the path, where feet go.

Leave the open fields, where beasts and machines move unimpeded, and where each thing knows its familiar scale. Step across this shaded threshold, step through the tall green door, into a hall of majestic beings, extravagantly, impossibly huge beings: mostly upright, reaching into lofty canopies, some horizontal, reaching down to remember hidden earth, some leaning, slanting, many embracing, entwining. Slow steps in a great intricate, intimate dance, heavy, and rooted. Now where, or how, can you walk? Every way you turn is blocked by immense moss-soft forms. You are stopped. You wait. You listen.

You slide sideways, from familiar measured time into a province of softened edges, breathing to an older rhythm. Not so much that time slows, or ceases altogether to move. More that senses still, and you notice that time, like noise, has been left out there somewhere, belongs to that other world.

I remember sinking into brilliant mosses--even in the filtered light they glowed--luxurious cushions and pillows, under hand, under foot. And, reaching down from overhead, festooning garlands of greens, with silver-grays.

Great-girthed substantial citizens--cedars, hemlocks, firs-- tentacle-rooted in and over the yielding bodies of their still larger deceased elders.

I remember scrambling up onto massive horizontal trunks, using them for walkways, for bridges, peering down from them, into pools of dark still water.

I remember thinking: one could disappear here, be ingested, be dissolved into this gathering of green. A part of me wanted this ingestion, reached out to it, prepared to give over to it.

I do not remember finding my way back out into sun, into the expectant puppy-tongue enthusiasm of the real-estate agent. But I remember his pitch, pouring over me:

> ...rare opportunity... last of its kind... valuable old-growth timber....
> The value of the timber alone is as much as the asking price for the parcel....

On and on, the recitation. Could I see how easy it was? How I should simply log it and have my cleared land, paid for, ready to farm? Easy, easy, easy!

My stunned sensibilities struggled to absorb the shock. I had been, before that day, in many lovely forests: in the Rockies, and the eastern provinces, in England, Bangladesh, Brazil. And, of course, I had walked, consciously and unconsciously, where mighty forests once stood, and stand no longer. But no loss pushed so hard into my own root as this. So, like others before me, I found myself taken by the passion and the grief for old-growth temperate rainforest.

A few days later I bought my farm, not far away. An old farmhouse, a tumble-down barn. A decadent orchard, some cleared fields in rough pasture, some second and third-growth forest. Sometime around the turn of the century, this too had been ancient forest. A scattering of mighty gray-beard snags and stumps remained, remnants of nurse logs, massive as great Biblical fishes (they yet may last for hundreds of years): in these fragments, as in faded, fragile pages, an old story called to memory.

And what of that hushed cathedral, that scrap of dark-mother forest, into which I had so briefly, unexpectedly entered, that sunny afternoon, as into an archaic enchantment? I did not enter her again. Within weeks she existed only in memory. Perhaps only in my memory. In her place was cleared land subdivided into "affordable" little acreages. And folks came eagerly from the city to purchase their parcels of rural tranquillity.

Very much like me.

* * *

This morning--most mornings--I stand for a moment at the door of my workshop, looking toward the creek. Between me and the sound of water, cedar branches, glossed by sunlight, are looping down in elegant lacy curtains. Walking under them, I pause to brush their flat waxy fingers with mine. I put my nose to their aromatic tips.

These cedars are youngsters. Even the stumps from the most recent logging are mostly from trees which stood less than a hundred years. Infants and children, in the tribe of trees.

It is said that, if undisturbed, cedars typically live to a thousand years, and that exceptional elders can live to two thousand. So I imagine-- a little romantic reverie--that somewhere up-coast, north of here, in a remote hidden cove stands an ancient grove, and, protected by it, a great ancestor cedar birthed in the same year as the baby of Bethlehem. Such a venerable one is not to be found on our island, where the current logging frenzy is the second, and in some places, the third wave, since the small farm clearings of the European settlers around the turn of the last century. It is said that before the settlers, in this somewhat drier rainshadow of the coastal zone, there were fires, every 500 years or so. But the old veterans can live through those fires, so the settlers would have known them.

I guess these Europeans, armed with axes and handsaws, had some struggle with the old leviathan survivors. Stories tell that when they brought one of these giants down they had no way to move it, so they would burn it where it fell, a process of many days. One can imagine that once upon a time this clearing of old growth for farms was a kind of heroism.

This house where I live, this workshop and garden, and the neighbors' house and garden: where all of them stand one of the settler families once farmed, or tried to farm. Walking in the young forest that has grown up again, you stumble onto decayed and rusted remnants--ghosts and whispers--of old buildings, old machinery.

There are a few charred witnesses of the fires. A stump ten or twelve feet high, burned out inside, crouching in the undergrowth like a monsterized spider. A still-living gnarly fir, its blackened cavity large enough to crawl into, for shelter or a seance.

* * *

Someone asked me--how long have you been talking to trees?--and I didn't know the answer. I tried to remember, working back along the chain of memory, hand over hand, link by link. When did this conversation begin?

In a memory fragment that floats up just now I am a Salish woman, gathering cedar bark for a basket, for a rain hat, for a cloak. As I choose a tree, as I begin to take strips of bark, I am thanking:

> "Grandmother, I come to ask for a small piece of your garment ... for I am going to make a basket, for berries...."

Western Red Cedar. You are the one called Medicine Tree, and Helper Tree. Today I find a dozen uses for you, but to the people native to these shores you gave a thousand gifts. The gifts of shelter, first of all. Planks, for the great long-houses, and carved poles at their entrances. Then the water gifts: canoes, paddles, harpoons, and hooks. Homely gifts: benches, boxes, and baskets. Ceremonial gifts: masks, rattles, drums. Clothing and towels, dishes and diapers, a list that is a litany, cradle to coffin. To stand next to you for a few moments, it is said, is to partake of your giftedness. To lean on you is to become like you in generosity. I wonder if the medicine still works.

Another memory trace, a primal fragment, perhaps older than the Salish or the Haida: I look up through limbs that are the Shaman's ladder, aspiring to the airy heights. To wisdom perhaps? To spirit power? A prayer, a chant: let me soar with the falcon; take me to the bright source.

Tree of Life. Pillar of Heaven. World Tree.

You are the one whom Jesus adorns. And Odin. And Quetzalcoatl. You are the one who is Mother Isis, offering to us her many fruits. You, with the spirit bird in your hair. You, with the shaggy wolf gnawing at your foot. A seeker reaches for your golden apple, aspires to be worn in your crown. But today the crown is not for me. I sink into forest litter, groping with the slenderest of your root-tip filaments toward a darker secret. I am a cub. Apprentice me to the ancient wolf.

* * *

So, I am not as much inclined to talk as I once was. What is to say? Can it be said in silence?

Perhaps the real question is not about talking to trees, but about listening. Their voices are unobtrusive. I never hear them moralize. Approach them with a chain saw, and they go in minutes. There is a groaning. A cracking. A sighing shudder. There is a great, long, whooshing exhalation, before the massive slam of wood on earth... and the air vibrates afterwards.

At the ferry landing, waiting in the lineup to leave our island, there will be two, or perhaps three, truckloads of logs.

A dream persists, even yet, that before all are gone we will be able to buy some bits and pieces of the present forest, to let it be. A dream that on this smallish island a forest may again grow very very old. And each day, at the landing, such a dream grows more tenuous, stretches to gossamer.

For the few moments it takes to cross the water I stand with my hand on the butt of a venerable lady. I could count her rings if I wanted to and know her age, but perhaps that would be intrusive. I do not count. I whisper (not audibly) an apology, and a farewell. Surprising me, she will have no truck with my melancholy.

"Hey, boy, its an adventure!" she admonishes. "Time for me to get out and see something of the world. This is the smartest way to go--let *them* buy the ticket. I'm thinking maybe I'd like to see the old temples at Kyoto. Or perhaps that fancy new airport at Hong Kong. I'm going incognito, you know, disguised as a pallet of 10 x 12's. Cheer up now! I'll send a post card."

I am non-plussed by such levity where I had expected the shared solemnity of endings, of loss. I get back into my car and the ferry unloads. The load of logs turns south. I turn north.

* * *

I too own a chainsaw.

After the loggers had taken what they wanted and an acre of their debris was mine I took down some of the small trees that remained to build my sheds, to give sun to a garden spot, to make this bright courtyard at my workshop. I left the trees that shade the stream and paths, and the ones that screen us from the road. The mosaic that this island is, of cleared and wooded spaces, creates lots of edges, is paradise for deer, for songbirds, for humans of my tribe.

Is it that we can abide the young trees, and the mini groves, but the grand ones make us mad?

Crossing the courtyard, I follow the short path down to the water and, under the draped tapestries, into a green sanctuary, a miniature chapel, that miraculously remains here after fires and farmers have come and gone, after three generations of loggers have taken their bounty, after I have followed footstep in footstep.

It is cool, dark, and verdant here, under the low canopy. It is no cathedral. But it is here that I come when I might want to remember the cathedrals. A bulking memory remains here of those soaring heights, of the layered light as from high leaded windows, of the ancient hush. This tangible memory is a gray and green-mossed massive cedar stump.

I do not notice you at first, Old One--so shadowed you are, so grown-about. So disconcertingly huge. When I do see you, when my eyes finally focus and acknowledge what they are seeing, you are an astonishment, a dominance.

You are twice as tall as I am up to that level where, above your rooted swell, a very long two-man saw whispered through you. Back then, when I was a child, or not even conceived. Two sets of square toe notches, one above the other, on your two flanks. The lowest notch for climbing up; the higher for standing in, to do the sawing.

Woodpeckers have since decorated you with additional holes and notches: rounds, and squares, and rectangles, and a sprinkle of fresh chips from their most recent hammering.

Out of the top of you grow a hemlock and two young cedars, a trio of juveniles. They have sent exploring roots down over you into the ground, thickening from ropes to muscular legs. One suspects there may be also some roots groping down through the dark belly of you, into earth. Huckleberries too, grow from you, high over my head. And salal, brambles, swordfern, the familiar green bouquet.

It is a disorientation to look up to them, as if our little planet is tipped on its edge.

12. RAVEN

September mornings.

Even before the rains come, or the leaves turn, you know. You walk out of the door, and summer is ended.

An expectancy? No, it has already happened. There is a different quality, and you know it. A change of light? An odor? A hush, before the winds that will be sweeping up the channel from the south-east? Before it is tangible, the body has shifted with the shift of season. The body has alerted, tingles to it.

Later, the maple leaves, touched by the mythical king, will begin to be beaten sheets of metal. At last, after the time that was dry and heat-heavy, will return the music and the dancing. Leaves, fir tips, flung packets of rain, a swelling stream: all will remember the dance... sedate at first, later a frenzy. But, before any of that buzz, that busy motion and commotion, one clear, still, September morning, I walk out of my door, and I hear the ravens.

That is how I know. If I was un-attuned to subtler signals, this is the one I cannot miss. This is the one I look for, listen for, and love.

The gathering of ravens.

A season has turned.

Some say Raven's story is about blackness. Some say it is mischief. Some say play; some, transformation. I say, listen to the music. Listen for the clear-water note, the bell note. Listen for the song of autumn.

Year-round--any season at all--we have the little-brother crows. They are always here, and always raucous. Their caws, their croaks, their officiousness. Always reporting, always gibing. Do not mistake them for the raven. When you hear those two lovely bell-like tones you will know. But try to reproduce them, try to describe them, and you will be tongue-tied. I say, it is deep liquid. A kind of musical gulping, from the toes. Or, gargling with a silver ball in the throat. The Alaskan says it signals coming rain: "the water call, all harmonious and pleasing." But these poor, second-hand attempts, fall short. Go direct to the source, in September.

There is also, of course, the rest of Raven's impressive repertoire.
All of his barks, yells, clicks, and claps. His *arghs*, *kraacks*, *krawks*, and
gwaaks. His hooting whoop as he slides over, at treetop level. In language,
as in tricks, he is endlessly inventive. A constant comment: to himself, to
the company of ravens, to crows if necessary, to the sky. "An intricate and
versatile language," the scientist says, "specific to purposes and
occasions." And, at the end, do not fail to mention the solid *whuush*,
whuush, *whuush*, of Raven's spread fingers on the air. You will always look
up, when you hear it.

* * *

Playtime. Look!--a couple of ravens are amusing themselves by
stealing the dog's bone. One of them attacks his tail; when he drops the
bone, the other flies off with it. Then or later you may hear the drift of
mocking laughter. Raven is like that. Tell your Aunt Bessie to watch out:
he'll have her special teaspoons.

You will see ravens passing objects back and forth for fun: a
shell, a bit of fur, a thimble. They will drop a twig in the air and catch it as
it falls. They will play goofy, hanging from a branch by their feet, or even
by their bills. Of course they will always find new and annoying things to
filch. An egg, a careless bracelet or ring, your lunch. A golf course swears
8000 balls carried off in a season.

Aerial play is a favorite. Raven is harassing an eagle, diving from
above to strike him on the back. Is he pummeling? Clawing? Just teasing?
An eagle feather floats down. The part of the great white-headed raptor
seems heavy and ponderous, in this improbable duet. The flapping of his

huge wings feels labored. After a few more dive displays Raven wheels away, tossing over his shoulder a hoot of derision.

Sometimes sky play looks like a mating dance. I watched one raven overtake another, from behind and slightly above, and I thought it was a he coming in close to couple with a she. But, just an inch before contact—did I really see this?--she reversed in midair, like a black hummingbird, and he overshot her, a black bullet. He didn't sulk. They flew up companionably into a wide blue gymnasium, and practiced their aerobatics. They did somersaults, back-flips, wing-tuck rolls--doubles and triples--then some kick turns, like swim racers at the end of the pool, and finally some upside-down flying, as if they were stunt pilots in an old air show half a century ago.

This is sheer exuberance. This is nothing to do with courtship, I think, unless they are courting gravity, and wind. Nothing to do with food, nor with attack and defense. Simply the rising of the sap, the urge, the yeast. A poet sings to it: "winged energy of delight."

* * *

Here on his Northwest coast Raven is in charge. He creates the place: these islands, the rivers, the people. But it isn't quite that simple. He doesn't really intend to make the rivers; the water just spills out of his bill. Besides, it is stolen from his friend Petrel, which explains how Raven's fine white feathers get to be scorched black. That happens when he is trying to escape through Petrel's smoke hole with a big beakfull of water, and the Smoke Hole Spirits are hauling him back down by his feet, and Petrel--pretty damn mad--is throwing pitchy wood on the fire. So now Raven is black all over, but he pretends he doesn't care. "Oh," he says, "black's a good color. I think it makes me handsomer than ever. And them white feathers was hard to keep up." And off he goes.

Raven is a gift-giver but it looks like most of his gifts are the inadvertent fruits of his looting and mischief. He is always busy amusing himself, preening his ego, playing shaman, playing the fool. To get the sun and moon up into the sky he has to steal them from the sly old fellow who has been keeping them all this time in his treasure box, and to accomplish that requires months of elaborate lying and chicanery. Starting of course--with seduction of the beautiful daughter. Even then, Raven would have flown off with the bright lights and kept them for himself if Eagle hadn't swooped in and beat up on him, made him let go of them. More often than not Raven's trickster habits bring him to a nasty pass--he is repeatedly swallowed, dismembered, shat on--and painfully he puts himself back together again.

It seems as if people have been annoyed at Raven for as long as we have memory and stories. In another part of the world, old Noah gets mad at him because he doesn't return to the ark as instructed, with news of dry land. And Apollo is furious at him for tattling on the god's love interest, the fair Coronis.

In Germanic lore that old shape-shifter Odin keeps regular company with his two black messengers--ravens of course--named Thought and Memory. What are they up to, flying about the world? Checking on fights and disasters? Gathering gossip? When they return they sit on his shoulders and whisper in his ears what they have seen and heard. His personal news channel and internet? No. Odin is one who is looking for wisdom. He is ready to put out one of his eyes if that will help open his inner eye. So Raven, it would seem, is the deep messenger, the one who brings intimations from the other side. He seems to be my shadow, gesturing in the direction I have feared to look.

A pod will swell, will be great with seed, and refuse to burst. November rains turn it slimy with black mold. Two dusky shapes sit hunched on the rail, shuffling and ruffling their feathers in a wet wind.

I am sitting at my kitchen table, drinking coffee, and for a moment the air darkens. A gust of rain slaps the window. The cup has gone cold in my hands... the ring of the telephone is startling, a summons... the lover suddenly looks away....

You think you hear a dog howling, and it will be Raven. The black joker can imitate a hen's proud cackle, or a baby's wail. If he wants to, he may recite battle scenes from the Iliad, or a somber line from Poe.

A woman gets up out of her bed, leaves her husband and her children sleeping, takes a ship to Samoa and paints tropical canvases full of somber foliage and dark crimson fruit.

True, we have heard the poet sing his love for the day, for the sun on the mountain. But he knows that half of his life, the slippery irreducible half, belongs to the wild darkness. The whetstone to his blade is the allure of oblivion, the odium and terror of betrayal. He knows he is just this tiny moment of incandescence, bursting like a sparkler, against a sable sky. He knows he is in the mouth of the great moth, soon to be sucked up with all of this little light.

Dark nights, in the guise of a crusty graybeard, Odin still walks the earth, door to door, hearth to hearth, shadowing his face with the collar of his dusty cloak. The old hermit pauses at the corner of an ordinary street, looks right, looks left.

So are we pulled to your darkness, Raven, to that beard of black feathers at your throat. So, it may be, to our shadow selves. We have followed you to the wars--how many tribes and countries? To the black hole of fostered enmities and revenge. Sorrow, black as Raven's wing, announcing the Dark Angel, bearing her gift. Any chasm into which we may slide or tumble: the pitchy bag of shame, the guilty midnight thrill of evil. That glimpse into whatever void or presence it is, unspeakable, beyond all the darknesses we can wrap our words about.

Oh, if we could fly with you, Messenger, through the crack between the worlds! We call this world round, but where it gapes into that other, it feels sharp as the edge of a knife. Is it to blunt that keenest edge that we have called you Trickster? Well, I seem to be here to learn your tricks. And I have an apprehension; I may not like them.

Is it true that if I am too solemn you will come in the night and steal my cattle? Sleep with my wife? How many times has it happened already? How many life times?

There was the time I was hiking up-country and I asked you where I should camp. Oh, you led me to such a lovely meadow, bright with flowers, a chuckling stream... and during the night, while I slept, the side of the mountain roared down to bury me in my tent.

There was my dream just last night: I dreamt a desirable woman, smooth as water, supple as wind. Silver in moonlight we danced. Ecstatic in desire we moved together. As I embraced her she slid back the beauty that had hidden a blunt hooked beak, she laid aside the fair garment of skin that had covered your dusky feathers. And you laughed.

You get yourself chopped up, chewed up, spit up--and you laugh.

You get me tangled up in your skein of mischief, more often than not an embarrassment of bodily functions--and you laugh.

Is there anything else? Anything that is *not* your shape-shifting, and your joke? The Mantis, pretending to be the twig. The carefree hitchhiker, dressed up as a burr. That race of brainy beings who call your world their space ship--and imagine that they are at the controls. Jokes, and more jokes. All of them shining like a penny, until we come to the punch line.

In the fine print, it is written that the crouching forest mouse shall pounce on the scimitar owl.

* * *

Beside my door--imperious, presiding--you sit here on your branch, Dark Brother, and here is your gleaming eye still on me. Once upon a time we called you Oracle. So what is it that you are seeing, just now, with your oracle eye?

Down at the beach there is a mob scene, a lone raven swarmed by serious crows, and they beat and peck and tear at him until what remains is a slack pouch, a drift of stained feathers. In just that moment, before the light winks out, I think I am in there, looking out through your eye, and I see, or imagine I see, the great serpent-boat, rocking on the sea of milk, and a lotus bud arising from sleepy Vishnu's navel. For just such a glancing moment, Old Shaman, I pierce your masquerade--rogue, fool, demon-lover--to glimpse who is in there. Under that ironic cloak of personality, I think you may be more like a process. I see that you are the congealing of gases into galaxies and stars, the twist and spiral of DNA, an illuminated turn of phrase. It looks like you are blazing energy, echoing space, elegant indifference... and all the costumed dancers waiting to leap out of them.

For a fine joke, you shrink yourself down to raven size, hide yourself behind those shiny black feathers, and visit me, in autumn.

It was ages ago that a humorous Chinese sage noticed his enemy in the shape of his own shadow, the very shape that he cast, himself, upon the ground? Well, I am wondering about the shape of his friend, which, so far as I know, he did not mention.

I am thinking I should like to look at my shadow, any luminous day, and see old Raven strut.

Certainly I should like to imitate some of his aerial back-flips and somersaults, just for fun.

It would be good, I suppose, to find in my shadow a few fragments of Thought, some traces of Memory.

Some day--some other day--I might ask for a pair of beautiful black wings, to lift and dissolve into a beautiful dark sky. But if you ask me this moment for my wish I will say: let my shadow shape itself as a container, perhaps a well-woven basket of dusky reeds, large enough to hold two bright musical notes. Bell notes. Your water-call, Brother. Song of September.

13. MOON

You dream an amazing thing: dolphins leaping.

At first you dream only a hush-a-by sea mirrored with moonlight. A ripple and then the spreading of thick watery folds presenting a dolphin snout, a dolphin grin, a gleaming dolphin forehead. He holds your eye for a moment, and disappears. A liquid explosion and out of it a dolphin leaping, sleek as surprise, weightless as melody.

Far across diamond water another dolphin levitates and splashes. Another and another--closer, further, faster--every way your eyes turn, everywhere an effervescence. Your ears are awash with the sound of splashing. Ever higher the leaping, impossibly high, until they are spinning hundreds of feet in the air: a melee of cavorting and cartwheeling; an ecstatic carousel. Once in a lifetime you may be looking up into the night when she showers you with star dust. Once, under a lucky moon, you may see the ocean dance.

You wake, and your room is flooded with moon luster. Go to the window and look down, to your own garden, silvered, serene. The fish pool is dark but the miniature waterfall winks and flashes. The rose arbor gleams: your tiny old-fashioned roses, a thousand pale moths. Paths, stones, beds, apple trees: all are washed with an ivory enchantment. Calling you. Calling you.

Quick, then, into your silver slippers. Fly down the stairs and out, your hair a streaming halo. Dance the glimmering paths. Dance the iris spears, the poppies and honeysuckle, but most of all, dance the moon-brushed lilies. Pause amongst them, to savor their night fragrances. Lean down to touch their confident flared elegance, to stroke their waxy curves. Glowing Madonnas, Regals, White Tigers, and--magnificent enough for heraldic angels at heaven's gate--these splendid Trumpets.

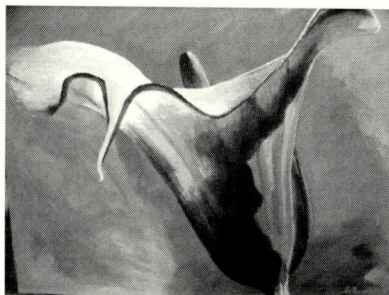

Night voices; sky is resonating; music of the spheres. Go to the music. Run, fly, dance, out of the garden gate, through the shadowy lane, down the familiar path to the beach. Light steps, across illuminated sand, to rocks and whispering water. Night air sensuous, a lover's breath on your skin. Moon high, her sea-path a slender crinkly ribbon. Wade in, and she will caress you.

* * *

If Wonder should let herself be captured, perhaps only for a moment, I could make a short list of amazing wonderful things! I think I would begin it with you Selene. You--small, circling rock in our sky--and the invisible strands that bind you to us.

How often have I watched you rise--fat, fire-orange, and near-- over our sister island, and reached out to receive, to contain (as if I were a bowl or a basket) the rush of your beauty! Yet again, in the cool hour before dawn, who has not looked up to your tiny remote white stillness, to be struck with wordless yearning? Who has not been plucked, a taut and vibrant string?

Can it be true that moon-struck adventurers of my clan set off on a voyage to you, landed a craft on your perilous shore? Is it true that we put our footprint on your flank, and left our space litter on your face? Did we dream this thing, or do it? And if we did it, where under heaven did we gather the spiral energy to fly out to you?

We imagine a robust sun god reaching out his long muscular arms toward us, and we reach out our slender earth arms and join hands, and he spins us. Then we reach out our other arms to you, silver lady, and you reach back and everybody holds tight and the music plays and everybody spins. And we, irrepressible earth monkeys, use all this fine spin to fling ourselves out to you, oh yes, beyond you, into the dance of the martial god, the jovial god, the cosmic saturnalia.... Up and out. A galaxy is large. It is said that in its dance are a trillion moons.

Surely all this reaching out is an awesome thing, excellent, and full of wonder. And then there is the reaching down, the looking in.

Is there truth, old Moon Mother, in the rumor that, far as you are, you are mistress of tides, in oceans and in us? Can it be true that moon cycles and woman cycles interweave as a single cloth? How? Why? Then there is that fine fancy, White Goddess, that you birth in us the muse! It is, I suppose, no further fetch, to imagine that you gift us with those twin enchantments, love and lunacy. Ah yes, Luna! We like to spin our magical stories around you, but before we knew how to spin, either wool or stories, already you had woven us into the tapestry of your waxing and your waning.

Beside you, Moon, on my list of amazing things, I would have to put reflection.

How is it that those intrepid ones who went up to visit you came back and told me that they walked on gray dust? That is not what I see. I remain dazzled, dazzled always, by the brilliance of your dresses: your harvest gold, blood orange, frost white, and quicksilver. I am captivated by that marvel, that astonishing bounce, the fusillade, that we call light. How is it, old stone, that you can capture those speeding photons as they rush by, can turn them about to a new assignation, to find so effortlessly my eye?

And where do such little bright packets go when my eye is closed? Where are they just now, as I am seeing them zipping about in my mind's eye? Moon and mind, dark and bright together, interwoven stems from a single root. *Mene*--the moon, in the old languages. *Mene*--the root from which grow number, measure, the calendar, and writing. All birthed of *mene*, of mind. *Mental.* All birthed of the *menses*: the cycle, the ebb and the flow.

So here is light, reflected in my twin mirrors, eye and mind. The astonishment of seeing anything: a star or a paradox, a leaf, an enigma. But, after all, perhaps these radiant things, light and reflection, moon and mind, are no more amazing than the dark ocean out of which they leap. Stopping now to think about it, what could I possibly mean by naming one thing *most amazing*, as if the shadowed womb behind it could fail to astonish. As if the mystery of the un-namable matrix were not the primal mind bender.

A gibbous moon has, for the past quarter hour, tethered herself to the black branches of the big fir at the end of the garden, waiting for me to notice... and to hush. As I look up, she unties the painter, and sails out into her mysterious sea.

* * *

In a charming image from West Africa, Mawu and Lisa, the heavenly twins, the lovers, are looking after things. Mawu is the woman, the moon, and she looks after the night. Lisa is the man, the sun, and he looks after the day. When there is an eclipse, they are making love. Eventually, they birth all the gods: earth gods, storm gods, iron gods, and the others.

Mawu, the mother, is most honored, for she brings us welcome relief from heat, brings life-giving moisture, offers her light in the dark, when it is most needed. Mawu is praised for her mystery, for her visible powers of dying and re-birthing.

She is the sexy one.

She is the pregnant one.

And she is the old snaggle witch with black teeth, the great devourer.

Of the paths we mortals may walk, here are two.

Here is Lisa's daylight path, so linear and clear. We like to think we walk it in wakefulness. We like to make of it a sunny highway. It is wide, it leads us away from the realm of the mothers. It tames the territories of ghosts and bears.

But here also is the left-hand path, which shimmers and moves under Mawu's pale light. Turn your face to the moon and you will be pushed by currents, pulled by tides. You will not walk. You will dance, you will drown, you will ride the ancient mare. Rafting on moon river you will not see around the bend.

The maenads will have you, will dismember you.

Your fingers will crawl, or scuttle, across the bottom of a briny sea.

Your heart will drift, in the loon's crazy cry, through wild northern spaces.

Your stretched and scaly toes will step the steps of the un-hurried heron, her old slow dance, before an audience of reeds.

* * *

High over my apple trees old Selene draws a translucent veil across her face. As I watch she encircles herself with a colored pulsating halo, a double rainbow. Moisture, minute prisms, the beads and jewels of her radiant gown. She hides. She reveals. She promises, and she remembers.

On some starlit path, love hurries toward breathless love.

In some silent moon-washed garden white trumpets are flaring.

Out over a silvered spread of sea, dolphins are leaping.